Bayard Taylor

Boys of Other Countries

Stories for American boys

Bayard Taylor

Boys of Other Countries
Stories for American boys

ISBN/EAN: 9783337427047

Printed in Europe, USA, Canada, Australia, Japan

Cover: Foto ©Andreas Hilbeck / pixelio.de

More available books at **www.hansebooks.com**

Boys of Other Countries

STORIES FOR AMERICAN BOYS

BY

BAYARD TAYLOR

ILLUSTRATED

NEW YORK

G. P. PUTNAM'S SONS

182 FIFTH AVENUE

1876

CONTENTS.

STORY I.

THE LITTLE POST-BOY.

IN my travels about the world I have made the acquaintance of a great many children, and I might tell you many things about their dress, their speech, and their habits of life, in the different countries I have visited. I presume, however, that you would rather hear me relate some of my adventures in which children partici-

1

pated, so that the story and the information shall
be given together. Ours is not the only country
in which children must frequently begin, at an
early age, to do their share of work and accustom
themselves to make their way in life. I have
found many instances among other races, and in
other climates, of youthful courage, and self-re-
liance, and strength of character, some of which I
propose to relate to you.

This one shall be the story of my adventure with
a little post-boy, in the northern part of Sweden.

Very few foreigners travel in Sweden in the
winter, on account of the intense cold. As you
go northward from Stockholm, the capital, the
country becomes ruder and wilder, and the climate more severe. In the sheltered valleys along
the Gulf of Bothnia and the rivers which empty
into it, there are farms and villages for a distance
of seven or eight hundred miles, after which fruit-
trees disappear, and nothing will grow in the
short, cold summers except potatoes and a little
barley. Farther inland, there are great forests
and lakes, and ranges of mountains where bears,
wolves, and herds of wild reindeer make their

home. No people could live in such a country unless they were very industrious and thrifty.

I made my journey in the winter, because I was on my way to Lapland, where it is easier to travel when the swamps and rivers are frozen, and the reindeer-sled can fly along over the smooth snow. It was very cold indeed, the greater part of the time: the days were short and dark, and if I had not found the people so kind, so cheerful, and so honest, I should have felt inclined to turn back more than once. But I do not think there are better people in the world than those who live in Norrland, which is a Swedish province, commencing about two hundred miles north of Stockholm.

They are a tall, strong race, with yellow hair and bright blue eyes, and the handsomest teeth I ever saw. They live plainly, but very comfortably, in snug wooden houses, with double windows and doors to keep out the cold; and since they cannot do much out-door work, they spin and weave and mend their farming implements in the large family room, thus enjoying the winter in spite of its severity. They are very happy and contented, and few of them would be willing to leave that cold country and make their homes in a warmer climate.

Here there are neither railroads nor stages, but the government has established post-stations at distances varying from ten to twenty miles. At each station a number of horses, and sometimes vehicles, are kept, but generally the traveller has his own sled, and simply hires the horses from one station to another. These horses are either furnished by the keeper of the station or some of the neighboring farmers, and when they are wanted a man or boy goes along with the traveller to bring them back. It would be quite an independent and convenient way of travelling, if the horses were always ready; but sometimes you must wait an hour or more before they can be furnished.

I had my own little sled, filled with hay and covered with reindeer-skins to keep me warm. So long as the weather was not too cold, it was very pleasant to speed along through the dark forests, over the frozen rivers, or past farm after farm in the sheltered valleys, up hill and down, until long after the stars came out, and then to get a warm supper in some dark-red post cottage, while the cheerful people sang or told stories around the fire. The cold increased a little every day, to be sure, but I became gradually accustomed to it, and soon began to fancy that the Arctic climate was not so difficult to endure as I had supposed. At first the thermometer fell to zero; then it went down ten degrees below; then twenty, and finally thirty. Being dressed in thick furs from head to foot, I did not suffer greatly; but I was very glad when the people assured me that such extreme cold never lasted more than two or three days. Boys of twelve or fourteen very often went with me to bring back their fathers' horses, and so long as those lively, red-cheeked fellows could face the weather, it would not do for me to be afraid.

One night there was a wonderful aurora in the sky. The streamers of red and blue light darted hither and thither, chasing each other up to the zenith and down again to the northern horizon, with a rapidity and a brilliance which I had never seen before. "There will be a storm soon," said

my post-boy; " one always comes after these
lights."

Next morning the sky was overcast, and the
short day was as dark as our twilight.   But it was
not quite so cold, and I travelled onward as fast
as possible.   There was a long tract of wild and
thinly settled country before me and I wished to
get through it before stopping for the night.
Unfortunately it happened that two lumber-merchants were travelling the same way, and had
taken the horses; so I was obliged to wait at the
stations until horses were brought from the neighboring farms.   This delayed me so much that at
seven o'clock in the evening I had still one more
station of three Swedish miles before reaching
the village where I intended to spend the night.
Now, a Swedish mile is nearly equal to seven
English, so that this station was at least twenty
miles long.

I decided to take supper while the horse was
eating his feed.   They had not expected any
more travellers at the station, and were not prepared.   The keeper had gone on with the two
lumber-merchants; but his wife—a friendly, rosy-

faced woman—prepared me some excellent coffee, potatoes, and stewed reindeer-meat, upon which I made a satisfactory meal. The house was on the border of a large, dark forest, and the roar of the icy northern wind in the trees seemed to increase while I waited in the warm room. I did not feel inclined to go forth into the wintry storm, but, having set my mind on reaching the village that night, I was loath to turn back.

"It is a bad night," said the woman, "and my husband will certainly stay at Umea until morning. His name is Niels Petersen, and I think you will find him at the post-house when you get there. Lars will take you, and they can come back together."

"Who is Lars?" I asked.

"My son," said she. "He is getting the horse ready. There is nobody else about the house to-night."

Just then the door opened, and in came Lars. He was about twelve years old; but his face was so rosy, his eyes so clear and round and blue, and his golden hair was blown back from his face in such silky curls, that he appeared to be even

younger.   I was surprised that his mother should
be willing to send him twenty miles through the
dark woods on such a night.

"Come here, Lars," I said.   Then I took him
by the hand, and asked, "Are you not afraid to
go so far to-night?"

He looked at me with wondering eyes, and
smiled; and his mother made haste to say: "You
need not fear, sir.   Lars is young; but he'll take
you safe enough.   If the storm does n't get worse,
you'll be at Umea by eleven o'clock."

I was again on the point of remaining; but
while I was deliberating with myself, the boy had
put on his overcoat of sheep-skin, tied the lappets
of his fur cap under his chin, and a thick woolen
scarf around his nose and mouth so that only the
round blue eyes were visible; and then his
mother took down the mittens of hare's fur from
the stove, where they had been hung to dry.
He put them on, took a short leather whip, and
was ready.

I wrapped myself in my furs, and we went out
together.   The driving snow cut me in the face
like needles, but Lars did not mind it in the least.

He jumped into the sled, which he had filled with
fresh, soft hay, tucked in the reindeer-skins at the
sides, and we cuddled together on the narrow seat,
making everything close and warm before we set
out. I could not see at all, when the door of the
house was shut, and the horse started on the journey. The night was dark, the snow blew inces-
santly, and the dark fir-trees roared all around us.
Lars, however, knew the way, and somehow or
other we kept the beaten track. He talked to the
horse so constantly and so cheerfully, that after a
while my own spirits began to rise, and the way
seemed neither so long nor so disagreeable.

"Ho there, Axel!" he would say. "Keep the
road,—not too far to the left. Well done. Here's
a level: now trot a bit."

So we went on,—sometimes up hill, sometimes
down hill,—for a long time, as it seemed. I
began to grow chilly, and even Lars handed me
the reins, while he swung and beat his arms to
keep the blood in circulation. He no longer sang
little songs and fragments of hymns, as when we
first set out; but he was not in the least alarmed,
or even impatient. Whenever I asked (as I did

1*

about every five minutes), "Are we nearly there?" he always answered, "a little farther."

Suddenly the wind seemed to increase.

"Ah," said he, "now I know where we are : it's one mile more." But one mile, you must remember, meant *seven*.

Lars checked the horse, and peered anxiously from side to side in the darkness. I looked also, but could see nothing.

"What is the matter?" I finally asked.

"We have got past the hills on the left," he said. "The country is open to the wind, and here the snow drifts worse than anywhere else on the road. If there have been no ploughs out to-night we'll have trouble."

You must know that the farmers along the road are obliged to turn out with their horses and oxen, and plough down the drifts, whenever the road is blocked up by a storm.

In less than a quarter of an hour we could see that the horse was sinking in the deep snow. He plunged bravely forward, but made scarcely any headway, and presently became so exhausted that he stood quite still. Lars and I arose from

the seat and looked around. For my part, I saw
nothing except some very indistinct shapes of
trees : there was no sign of an opening through
them. In a few minutes the horse started again,
and with great labor carried us a few yards
farther.

"Shall we get out and try to find the road?"
said I.

"It's no use," Lars answered. "In these new
drifts we would sink to the waist. Wait a little,
and we shall get through this one."

It was as he said. Another pull brought us
through the deep part of the drift, and we reached
a place where the snow was quite shallow. But
it was not the hard, smooth surface of the road :
we could feel that the ground was uneven, and
covered with roots and bushes. Bidding Axel
stand still, Lars jumped out of the sled, and began
wading around among the trees. Then I got out
on the other side, but had not proceeded ten
steps before I began to sink so deeply into the
loose snow that I was glad to extricate myself and
return. It was a desperate situation, and I wondered how we should ever get out of it.

I shouted to Lars, in order to guide him, and
it was not long before he also came back to the
sled. "If I knew where the road is," said he, "I
could get into it again. But I don't know; and I
think we must stay here all night."

"We shall freeze to death in an hour!" I
cried. I was already chilled to the bone. The
wind had made me very drowsy, and I knew that
if I slept I should soon be frozen.

"O, no!" exclaimed Lars, cheerfully. "I am
a Norrlander, and Norrlanders never freeze. I
went with the men to the bear-hunt, last winter,
up on the mountains, and we were several nights
in the snow. Besides, I know what my father did
with a gentleman from Stockholm on this very
road, and we'll do it to-night."

"What was it?"

"Let me take care of Axel first," said Lars.
"We can spare him some hay and one reindeer-
skin."

It was a slow and difficult task to unharness
the horse, but we accomplished it at last. Lars
then led him under the drooping branches of a
fir-tree, tied him to one of them, gave him an arm-

ful of hay, and fastened the reindeer-skin upon his back. Axel began to eat, as if perfectly satisfied with the arrangement. The Norrland horses are so accustomed to cold that they seem comfortable in a temperature where one of ours would freeze.

When this was done, Lars spread the remaining hay evenly over the bottom of the sled and covered it with the skins, which he tucked in very firmly on the side towards the wind. Then, lifting them on the other side, he said: " Now take off your fur coat, quick, lay it over the hay, and then creep under it."

I obeyed as rapidly as possible. For an instant I shuddered in the icy air; but the next moment I lay stretched in the bottom of the sled, sheltered from the storm. I held up the ends of the reindeer-skins while Lars took off his coat and crept in beside me. Then we drew the skins down and pressed the hay against them. When the wind seemed to be entirely excluded Lars said we must pull off our boots, untie our scarfs, and so loosen our clothes that they would not feel tight upon any part of the body. When this was done, and we lay close together, warming each other, I found that the chill gradually passed out of my blood.   My hands and feet were no longer numb ; a delightful feeling of comfort crept over me ; and I lay as snugly as in the best bed.   I was surprised to find that, although my head was covered, I did not feel stifled.   Enough air came in under the skins to prevent us from feeling oppressed.

There was barely room for the two of us to lie, with no chance of turning over or rolling about.   In five minutes, I think, we were asleep, and I dreamed of gathering peaches on a warm August day, at home.   In fact, I did not wake up thoroughly during the night ; neither did Lars, though it seemed to me that we both talked in our sleep.   But as I must have talked English and he Swedish, there could have been no connection between our remarks.   I remember that his warm, soft hair pressed against my chin, and that his feet reached no further than my knees. Just as I was beginning to feel a little cramped and stiff from lying so still I was suddenly aroused by the cold wind on my face.   Lars had risen up on his elbow, and was peeping out from under the skins.

"I think it must be near six o'clock," he said. "The sky is clear, and I can see the big star. We can start in another hour."

I felt so much refreshed that I was for setting out immediately; but Lars remarked, very sensibly, that it was not yet possible to find the road. While we were talking, Axel neighed.

"There they are!" cried Lars, and immediately began to put on his boots, his scarf and heavy coat. I did the same, and by the time we were ready we heard shouts and the crack of whips. We harnessed Axel to the sled, and proceeded slowly in the direction of the sounds, which came, as we presently saw, from a company of farmers, out thus early to plough the road. They had six pairs of horses geared to a wooden frame, something like the bow of a ship, pointed in front and spreading out to a breadth of ten or twelve feet. The machine not only cut through the drifts but packed the snow, leaving a good, solid road behind it. After it had passed, we sped along merrily in the cold morning twilight, and in little more than an hour reached the post-house at Umea, where we found Lars's father prepared to return home. He waited, nevertheless, until Lars had eaten a good warm breakfast, when I said good-bye to both, and went on towards Lapland.

Some weeks afterwards, on my return to Stockholm, I stopped at the same little station. This time the weather was mild and bright, and the father would have gone with me to the next post-house ; but I preferred to take my little bed-fellow and sled-fellow. He was so quiet and cheerful and fearless, that, although I had been nearly all over the world, and he had never been away from home,—although I was a man and he a young boy,—I felt that I had learned a lesson from him, and might probably learn many more, if I should know him better. We had a merry trip. of two or three hours, and then I took leave of Lars forever. He is no doubt still driving travellers over the road, a handsome, courageous, honest-hearted young man, perhaps with his own son growing up to take his place, and help some later stranger, like myself, through a winter storm.

STORY II.

THE PASHA'S SON.

 GOOD many years ago, I spent a winter in Africa. I had intended to go up the Nile only as far as Nubia, visiting the great temples and tombs of Thebes on the way; but when I had done all this, and passed beyond the cataracts at the southern boundary of Egypt, I found the journey so agreeable, so full of interest, and attended with so much less danger than I had supposed, that I determined to go on for a month or two longer, and penetrate as far as possible into the interior. Everything was favorable to my plan. I crossed the great Nubian Desert without accident or adventure, reached the ancient region of Ethiopia, and continued my journey until I had advanced beyond all the cataracts of the Nile, to the point where the two great branches of the river flow together.

This point, which you will find on your maps
in the country called Sennaar, bordering Abyssinia on the northwestern side, has become very
important within the last twenty or thirty years.
The Egyptians, after conquering the country,
established there their seat of government for all
that part of Africa, and very soon a large and
busy town arose where formerly there had only
been a few mud huts of the natives.   The town is
called Khartoum, and I suppose it must contain,
by this time, forty or fifty thousand inhabitants.
It is built on a sandy plain, studded here and
there with clumps of thorny trees.   On the east
side the Blue Nile, the source of which was discovered by the Scotch traveller Bruce, in the last
century, comes down clear and swift from the
mountains of Abyssinia ; on the west, the broad,
shallow, muddy current of the White Nile, which
rises in the great lakes discovered by Speke and
Baker within the last twenty years, makes its
appearance.   The two rivers meet just below the
town, and flow as a single stream to the Mediter-
ranean, a distance of fifteen hundred miles.

Formerly all this part of Africa was consid-

ered very wild, barbarous, and dangerous to the
traveller. But since it has been brought under
the rule of the Egyptian government, the people
have been forced to respect the lives and property
of strangers, and travelling has become compara-
tively safe. I soon grew so accustomed to the
ways of the inhabitants, that by the time I
reached Khartoum I felt quite at home among
them. My experience had already taught me
that, where a traveller is badly treated, it is generally his own fault. You must not despise a
people because they are ignorant, because their
habits are different, or because they sometimes
annoy you by a natural curiosity. I found that
by acting in a kind yet firm manner towards
them, and preserving my patience and good-na-
ture, even when it was tried by their slow and
careless ways, I avoided all trouble, and even
acquired their friendly good-will.

When I reached Khartoum, the Austrian Consul invited me to his house; and there I spent
three or four weeks, in that strange town, making
acquaintance with the Egyptian officers, the chiefs
of the desert tribes, and the former kings of the

different countries of Ethiopia. When I left my
boat, on arriving, and walked through the narrow
streets of Khartoum, between mud walls, very few
of which were even whitewashed, I thought it a
miserable place, and began to look out for some
garden where I might pitch my tent, rather than
live in one of those dirty-looking habitations.
The wall around the Consul's house was of mud
like the others; but when I entered I found
clean, handsome rooms, which furnished delightful shade and coolness during the heat of the day.
The roof was of palm-logs, covered with mud,
which the sun baked into a hard mass, so that the
house was in reality as good as a brick dwelling.
It was a great deal more comfortable than it appeared from the outside.

There were other features of the place, however, which it would be difficult to find anywhere
except in Central Africa. After I had taken pos-
session of my room, and eaten breakfast with my
host, I went out to look at the garden. On each
side of the steps leading down from the door
sat two apes, who barked and snapped at me.
The next thing I saw was a leopard tied to the

trunk of an orange-tree. I did not dare to go within reach of his rope, although I afterwards became well acquainted with him. A little farther, there was a pen full of gazelles and an antelope with immense horns; then two fierce, bristling hyenas; and at last, under a shed beside the stable, a full-grown lioness, sleeping in the shade. I was greatly surprised when the Consul went up to her, lifted up her head, opened her jaws so as to show the shining white tusks, and finally sat down upon her back.

She accepted these familiarities so good-naturedly that I made bold to pat her head also. In a day or two we were great friends; she would spring about with delight whenever she saw me, and would purr like a cat whenever I sat down upon her back. I spent an hour or two every day among the animals, and found them all easy to tame except the hyenas, which would gladly have bitten me if I had allowed them a chance. The leopard, one day, bit me slightly in the hand; but I punished him by pouring several buckets of water over him, and he was always very amiable after that. The beautiful little

gazelles would cluster around me, thrusting up
their noses into my hand, and saying, " *Wow !*
wow !" as plainly as I write it. But none of
these animals attracted me so much as the big
lioness. She was always good-humored, though
occasionally so lazy that she would not even open
her eyes when I sat down on her shoulder. She
would sometimes catch my foot in her paws as a
kitten catches a ball, and try to make a plaything
of it,—yet always without thrusting out her claws.
Once she opened her mouth, and gently took one
of my legs in her jaws for a moment; and the
very next instant she put out her tongue and
licked my hand. There seemed to be almost as
much of the dog as of the cat in her nature.
We all know, however, that there are differences
of character among animals, as there are among
men; and my favorite probably belonged to a
virtuous and respectable family of lions.

The day after my arrival I went with the Consul to visit the Pasha, who lived in a large mud
palace on the bank of the Blue Nile. He received
us very pleasantly, and invited us to take seats in
the shady court-yard. Here there was a huge

panther tied to one of the pillars, while a little lion, about eight months old, ran about perfectly loose. The Pasha called the latter, which came

THE HOUSE IN KHARTOUM.

springing and frisking towards him. " Now," said he, " we will have some fun." He then made the lion lie down behind one of the pillars, and called to one of the black boys to go across the court-yard on some errand. The lion lay quite still until the boy came opposite to the pillar, when

he sprang out and after him.   The boy ran, terri-
bly frightened; but the lion reached him in five
or six leaps, sprang upon his back and threw him
down, and then went back to the pillar as if quite
satisfied with his exploit.   Although the boy was
not hurt in the least, it seemed to me like a cruel
piece of fun.   The Pasha, nevertheless, laughed
very heartily, and told us that he had himself
trained the lion to frighten the boys.

Presently the little lion went away, and when
we came to look for him, we found him lying on
one of the tables in the kitchen of the palace,
apparently very much interested in watching the
cook.   The latter told us that the animal sometimes took small pieces of meat, but seemed to
know that it was not permitted, for he would run
away afterwards in great haste.   What I saw of
lions during my residence in Khartoum satisfied
me that they are not very difficult to tame,—only,
as they belong to the cat family, no dependence
can be placed on their continued good behavior.

Among the Egyptian officers in the city was a
Pasha named Rufah, who had been banished from
Egypt by the Viceroy.   He was a man of consid-

erable education and intelligence, and was very unhappy at being sent away from his home and family. The climate of Khartoum is very unhealthy, and this unfortunate Pasha had suffered greatly from fever. He was uncertain how long his exile would continue: he had been there already two years, and as all the letters directed to him passed through the hands of the officers of government, he was quite at a loss how to get any help from his friends. What he had done to cause his banishment, I could not ascertain; probably he did not know himself. There are no elections in those Eastern countries; the people have nothing to do with the choice of their own rulers. The latter are appointed by the Viceroy at his pleasure, and hold office only so long as he allows them. The envy or jealousy of one Pasha may lead to the ruin of another, without any fault on the part of the latter. Probably somebody else wanted Rufah Pasha's place, and slandered him to the Viceroy for the sake of getting him removed and exiled.

The unhappy man inspired my profound sympathy. Sometimes he would spend the evening

2

with the Consul and myself, because he felt safe, in our presence, to complain of the tyranny under which he suffered. When we met him at the houses of the other Egyptian officers, he was very careful not to talk on the subject, lest they should report the fact to the government.

Being a foreigner and a stranger, I never imagined that I could be of any service to Rufah Pasha. I did not speak the language well, I knew very little of the laws and regulations of the country, and moreover, I intended simply to pass through Egypt on my return. Nevertheless, one night, when we happened to be walking the streets together, he whispered that he had something special to say to me. Although it was bright moonlight, we had a native servant with us, to carry a lantern. The Pasha ordered the servant to walk on in advance; and a turn of the narrow, crooked streets soon hid him from our sight. Everything was quiet, except the rustling of the wind in the palm-trees which rose above the garden-walls.

"Now," said the Pasha, taking my hand, "now we can talk for a few minutes, without being overheard. I want you to do me a favor."

" Willingly," I answered, " if it is in my power."

" It will not give you much trouble," he said, " and may be of great service to me. I want you to take two letters to Egypt,—one to my son, who lives in the town of Tahtah, and one to Mr. Murray, the English Consul-General, whom you know. I cannot trust the Egyptian merchants, because, if these letters were opened and read, I might be kept here many years longer. If you deliver them safely, my friends will know how to assist me, and perhaps I may soon be allowed to return home."

I promised to deliver both letters with my own hands, and the Pasha parted from me in more cheerful spirits at the door of the Consul's house. After a few days I was ready to set out on the return journey; but, according to custom, I was first obliged to make farewell visits to all the officers of the government. It was very easy to apprise Rufah Pasha beforehand of my intention, and he had no difficulty in slipping the letters into my hand without the action being

observed by any one. I put them into my port-
folio, with my own letters and papers, where they
were entirely safe, and said nothing about the
matter to any one in Khartoum.

Although I was glad to leave that wild town,
with its burning climate, and retrace the long way
back to Egypt, across the Desert and down the
Nile, I felt very sorry at being obliged to take
leave forever of all my pets. The little gazelles
said, " *Wow ! wow !* " in answer to my " Good-
bye ; " the hyenas howled and tried to bite, just
as much as ever ; but the dear old lioness I know
would have been sorry if she could have understood that I was going. She frisked around me,
licked my hand, and I took her great tawny head
into my arms, and gave her a kiss. Since then I
have never had a lion for a pet, and may never
have one again. I must confess, I am sorry for
it ; for I still retain my love for lions (four-footed
ones, I mean) to this day.

Well, it was a long journey, and I should have
to write many days in order to describe it. I
should have to tell of fierce sand-storms in the
Desert ; of resting in palm-groves near the old

capital of Ethiopia; of plodding, day after day, through desolate landscapes, on the back of a camel, crossing stony ranges of mountains, to reach the Nile again, and then floating down with the current in an open boat. It was nearly two months before I could deliver the first of the Pasha's letters,—that which he had written to his son. The town of Tahtah is in Upper Egypt, near Siout; you will hardly find it on the maps. It stands on a little mound, several miles from the Nile, and is surrounded by the rich and beautiful plain which is every year overflowed by the river.

There was a head wind, and my boat could not proceed very fast; so I took my faithful servant, Achmet, and set out on foot, taking a path which led over the plain between beautiful wheat-fields and orchards of lemon-trees. In an hour or two we reached Tahtah,—a queer, dark old town, with high houses and narrow streets. The doors and balconies were of carved wood, and the windows were covered with lattices, so that no one could look in, although those inside could easily look out. There were a few sleepy merchants in the bazar, smoking their pipes and enjoying the

odors of cinnamon and dried roses which floated
in the air.

After some little inquiry, I found Rufah
Pasha's house, but was not admitted, because the
Egyptian women are not allowed to receive the
visits of strangers. There was a shaded en-
trance-hall, open to the street, where I was
requested to sit, while the black serving-woman
went to the school to bring the Pasha's son. She
first borrowed a pipe from one of the merchants
in the bazar, and brought it to me. Achmet and
I sat there, while the people of the town, who had
heard that we came from Khartoum and knew the
Pasha, gathered around to ask questions.

They were all very polite and friendly, and
seemed as glad to hear about the Pasha as if they
belonged to his family. In a quarter of an hour
the woman came back, followed by the Pasha's
son and the schoolmaster, who had dismissed his
school in order to hear the news. The boy was
about eleven years old, but tall of his age. He
had a fair face, and large dark eyes, and smiled
pleasantly when he saw me. If I had not known
something of the customs of the people, I should

have given him my hand, perhaps drawn him
between my knees, put an arm around his waist
and talked familiarly; but I thought it best to
wait and see how he would behave towards me.

He first made me a graceful salutation, just as
a man would have done, then took my hand and
gently touched it to his heart, lips, and forehead,
after which he took his seat on the high divan, or
bench, by my side. Here he again made a salutation, clapped his hands thrice, to summon the
woman, and ordered coffee to be brought.

"Is your Excellency in good health?" he asked.

"Very well, praised be Allah!" I answered.

"Has your Excellency any commands for me?
You have but to speak; you shall be obeyed."

"You are very kind," said I; "but I have
need of nothing. I bring you greetings from the
Pasha, your father, and this letter, which I promised him to deliver into your own hands."

Thereupon I handed him the letter, which he
laid to his heart and lips before opening. As he
found it a little difficult to read, he summoned the
schoolmaster, and they read it together in a
whisper.

In the mean time coffee was served in little
cups, and a very handsome pipe was brought by
somebody for my use. After he had read the
letter, the boy turned to me with his face a little
flushed, and his eyes sparkling, and said, " Will
your Excellency permit me to ask whether you
have another letter ? "

" Yes," I answered ; " but it is not to be delivered here."

" That is right," said he. " When will you
reach Cairo ? "

" It depends on the wind ; but I hope in seven
days from now."

The boy again whispered to the schoolmaster,
but presently they both nodded, as if satisfied, and
nothing more was said on the subject.

Some sherbet (which is nothing but lemonade
flavored with rose-water) and pomegranates were
then brought to me, and the boy asked whether I
would not honor him by remaining during the
rest of the day. If I had not seen his face, I
should have supposed I was visiting a man,—so.
dignified and self-possessed and graceful was the
little fellow. The people looked on as if they

were quite accustomed to such mature manners
in children. I was obliged to use as much cere-
mony with the child as if he had been the governor of the town. But he interested me, nevertheless, and I felt curious to know the subject of his
consultation with the schoolmaster. I was sure
they were forming some plan to have the Pasha
recalled from exile.

After two or three hours I left, in order to
overtake my boat, which was slowly working its
way down the Nile. The boy arose, and walked
by my side to the end of the town, the other people. following us. When we came out upon the
plain, he took leave of me with the same saluta-
tions, and the words, " May God grant your Excellency a prosperous journey ! "

" May God grant it ! " I responded ; and all
the people repeated, " May God grant it ! "

The whole interview seemed to me like a
scene out of the " Arabian Nights." To me it
was a pretty, picturesque experience, which cannot be forgotten : to the people, no doubt, it was
an every-day matter.

When I reached Cairo, I delivered the other
2*

letter, and in a fortnight afterwards left Egypt; so that I could not ascertain, at the time, whether anything had been done to forward the Pasha's hopes. Some months afterwards, however, I read in a European newspaper, quite accidentally, that Rufah Pasha had returned to Egypt from Khartoum. I was delighted with the news; and I shall always believe, and insist upon it, that the Pasha's wise and dignified little son had a hand in bringing about the fortunate result.

STORY III.

JON OF ICELAND.

I.

THE boys of Iceland must be content with very few acquaintances and playmates. The valleys which produce grass enough for the farmer's ponies, cattle and sheep, are generally scattered widely apart, divided by ridges of lava so hard and cold that only a few wild flowers succeed in growing in their cracks and hollows. Then, since the farms must be all the larger, because the grass is short and grows slowly in such a severe northern climate, the dwellings are rarely nearer than four or five miles apart; and were it not for their swift and nimble ponies, the people would see very little of each other except on Sundays, when they ride long distances to attend worship in their little wooden churches.

But of all boys in the island, not one was so

lonely in his situation as Jon Sigurdson. His
father lived many miles beyond that broad, grassy
plain which stretches from the Geysers to the sea,
on the banks of the swift river Thiörva. On each
side there were mountains so black and bare that
they looked like gigantic piles of coal; but the
valley opened to the southward as if to let the
sun in, and far away, when the weather was clear,
the snowy top of Mount Hecla shone against the
sky. The farmer Sigurd, Jon's father, was a poor
man, or he would not have settled so far away
from any neighbors; for he was of a cheerful and
social nature, and there were few at Kyrkedal who
could vie with him in knowledge of the ancient
history and literature of Iceland.

The house was built on a knoll, under a cliff
which sheltered it from the violent west and
northwest winds. The walls, of lava stones and
turf, were low and broad; and the roofs over
dwelling, storehouses, and stables were covered
deep with earth, upon which grew such excellent
grass that the ponies were fond of climbing up
the sloping corners of the wall in order to get at
it. Sometimes they might be seen, cunningly

Jon's Home.

balanced on the steep sides of the roof, gazing along the very ridge-poles, or looking over the end of the gable when some member of the family came out of the door, as much as to say " Get me down if you can!" ·Around the buildings there was a square wall of inclosure, giving the place the appearance of a little fortress.

On one side of the knoll a hot spring bubbled up. In the morning or evening, when the air was cool, quite a little column of steam arose from it, whirling and broadening as it melted away; but the water was pure and wholesome as soon as it became cold enough for use. In front of the house, where the sun shone warmest, Sigurd had laid out a small garden. It was a great labor for him to remove the huge stones and roll them into a protecting wall, to carry good soil from the places where the mountain rills had gradually washed it down from above, and to arrange it so that frosts and cold rains should do the least harm; and the whole family thought themselves suddenly rich, one summer, when they pulled their first radishes, saw the little bed of potatoes coming into blossom, and the cabbages rolling up their leaves, in order to make, at least, baby-heads before the winter came.

Within the house, all was low, and dark, and dismal. The air was very close and bad, for the stables were only separated from the dwelling-room by a narrow passage, and bunches of dry, salt fish hung on the walls. Besides, it was usually full of smoke from the fire of peat, and, after a rain, of steam from Sigurd's and Jon's heavy woolen coats. But to the boy it was a delightful, a comfortable home, for within it he found shelter, warmth, food and instruction. The room for visitors seemed to him the most splen-did place in the world, because it had a wooden floor, a window with six panes of glass, a colored print of the King of Denmark, and a geranium in a pot. This was so precious a plant that Jon and his sister Gudrid hardly dared to touch its leaves. They were almost afraid to smell it, for fear of sniffing away some of its life; and Gudrid, after seeing a leaf of it laid on her dead sister's bosom, insisted that some angel, many hundred years ago, had brought the seed straight down from heaven.

These were Sigurd's only children. There
had been several more, but they had died in
infancy, from the want of light and pure air, and
the great distance from help when sickness came.
Gudrid was still pale and slender, except in summer, when her mild, friendly face took color from
the sun ; but Jon, who was now fourteen, was a
sturdy, broad-breasted boy, who promised to be as
strong as his father in a few years more. He had
thick yellow hair, curling a little around his forehead ; large, bright blue eyes; and a mouth
rather too broad for beauty, if the lips had not
been so rosy and the teeth so white and firm.
He had a serious look, but it was only because
he smiled with his eyes oftener than with his
mouth. He was naturally true and good, for he
hardly knew what evil was. Except his parents
and his sister, he saw no one for weeks at a time ;
and when he met other boys after church at
Kyrkedal, so much time always was lost in shyly
looking at each other and shrinking from the talk
which each wanted to begin, that no very intimate
acquaintance followed.

But, in spite of his lonely life, Jon was far from

being ignorant. There were the long winter months, when the ponies—and sometimes the sheep—pawed holes in the snow in order to reach the grass on the bottoms beside the river; when the cows were warmly stabled and content with their meals of boiled hay; when the needful work of the day could be done in an hour or two, and then Sigurd sat down to teach his children, while their mother spun or knit beside them, and from time to time took part in the instruction. Jon could already read and write so well that the pastor at Kyrkedal lent him many an old Icelandic legend to copy; he knew the history of the island, as well as that of Norway and Denmark, and could answer (with a good deal of blushing) when he was addressed in Latin. He also knew something of the world, and its different countries and climates; but this knowledge seemed to him like a strange dream, or like something that happened long ago and never could happen again. He was accustomed to hear a little birch-bush, four or five feet high, called " a tree," and he could not imagine how any tree could be a hundred feet high, or bear flowers and fruit. Once, a

trader from Rejkiavik—the chief seaport of Iceland—brought a few oranges to Kyrkedal, and
Sigurd purchased one for Jon and Gudrid. The
children kept it day after day, never tired of
enjoying the splendid color and strange, delightful perfume; so when they decided to cut the
rind at last, the pulp was dried up and tasteless.
A city was something of which Jon could form no
conception, for he had never even seen Rejkiavik; he imagined that palaces and cathedrals
were like large Icelandic farm-houses, with very
few windows, and turf growing on the roofs.

SIGURD'S wealth, if it could be called so, was in a small flock of sheep, the pasture for which was scattered in patches for miles up and down the river. The care of these sheep had been intrusted chiefly to Jon, ever since he was eight years old, and he had learned their natures and ways—their simple animal virtues and silly animal vices—so thoroughly, that they acquired a great respect for him, and very rarely tried to be disobedient. Even Thor, the ram, although he sometimes snorted and tossed his horns in protest, or stamped impatiently with his fore-feet, heeded his master's voice. In fact, the sheep became Jon's companions, in the absence of human ones; he talked to them so much during the lonely days, that it finally seemed as if they understood a great deal of his speech.

There was a rough bridle-path leading up the valley of the Thiörva ; but it was rarely travelled, for it struck northward into the cold, windy, stony desert which fills all the central part of Iceland. For a hundred and fifty miles there was no dwelling, no shelter from the fierce and sudden storms, and so little grass that the travellers who sometimes crossed the region ran the risk of losing their ponies from starvation. There were · lofty plains of black rock, as hard as iron ; groups of bare, snowy-headed mountains ; and often, at night, you could see a pillar of fire in the distance, showing that one of the many volcanoes was in action. Beyond this terrible wilderness the grassy valleys began again, and there were houses and herds, increasing as you came down to the bright.bays along the northern shore of the island.

More than once, a trader or Government messenger, after crossing the desert, had rested for a night under Sigurd's roof; and many were the tales of their adventures which Jon had treasured up in his memory. Sometimes they spoke of the *trolls* or mischievous fairies who came over with

the first settlers from Norway, and were still supposed by many persons to lurk among the dark
glens of Iceland. Both Sigurd and the pastor at
Kyrkedal had declared that there were no such
creatures, and Jon believed them faithfully ; yet
he could not help wondering as he sat upon some
rocky knoll overlooking his sheep, whether a
strange little figure *might* not come out of the
chasm opposite, and speak to him. The more he
heard of the terrors and dangers of the desert to
the northward, the more he longed to see them
with his own eyes and know them through his
own experience. He was not the least afraid ;
but he knew that his father would never allow
him to go alone, and to disobey a father was
something of which he had never heard, and
could not have believed to be possible.

When he was in his fifteenth year, however (it
was summer, and he was fourteen in April), there
came several weeks when no rain fell in the valley.
It was a lovely season for the garden ; even the
geranium in the window put forth twice as many
scarlet blossoms as ever before. Only the sheep
began to hunger ; for the best patch of grass in

front of the house was carefully kept for hay, and
the next best, further down the river, for the ponies.
So Jon was obliged to lead his flock to a narrow
little dell, which came down to the Thiörva, three
or four miles to the northward. Here, for a week,
they nibbled diligently wherever anything green
showed itself at the foot of the black rocks; and
when the pasture grew scanty again, they began
to stare at Jon in a way which many persons might
have thought stupid. *He* understood them; they
meant to say: "We've nearly finished this; find
us something more!"

That evening, as he was leading his flock into
the little inclosure beside the dwelling, he heard
his father and mother talking. He thought it no
harm to listen, for they had never said anything
that was not kind and friendly. It seemed, however, that they were speaking of him, and the very
first words he heard made his heart beat more
rapidly.

"Two days' journey away," said Sigurd; "are
excellent pastures that belong to nobody. There
is no sign of rain yet, and if we could send Jon
with the sheep — "

"Are you sure of it?" his wife asked.

"Eyvindur stopped to talk with me," he answered; "and he saw the place this morning. He says there were rains in the desert, and, indeed, I've thought so myself, because the river has not fallen; and he never knew as pleasant a season to cross the country."

"Jon might have to stay out a week or two; but, as you say, Sigurd, we should save our flock. The boy may be trusted, I'm sure; only, if anything should happen to him?"

"I don't think he's fearsome," said Sigurd; "and what should happen to him there, that might not happen nearer home?"

They moved away, while Jon clasped the palms of his hands hard against each other, and stood still for a minute to repeat to himself all he had heard. He knew Eyvindur, the tall, strong man with the dark curling hair, who rode the swift cream-colored pony, with black mane and tail. He knew what his father meant—nothing else than that he, Jon, should take the sheep two days' journey away, to the very edge of the terrible wilderness, and pasture them there, alone, probably, for many days! Why, Columbus, when he set sail from Palos, could not have had a brighter dream of unknown lands! Jon went in to supper in such a state of excitement that he hardly touched the dried fish and hard oaten bread; but he drank two huge bowls of milk and still felt thirsty. When, at last, Sigurd opened his lips and spake, and the mother sat silent with her eyes fixed upon her son's face, and Gudrid looked frightened, Jon straightened himself as if he were already a man, and quietly said: " I'll do it!"

He wanted to shout aloud for joy; but Gudrid began to cry.

However, when a thing had once been decided in the family, that was the end of any question or remonstrance, and even Gudrid forgot her fears in the interest of preparing a supply of food for Jon during his absence. They slept soundly for a few hours; and then, at two o'clock in the morning, when the sun was already shining on the snowy tops of the Arne Mountains, Jon hung the bag of provisions over his shoulder, kissed his parents and sister, and started northward, driving the sheep before him.

3

III.

IN a couple of hours he reached the farthest point of the valley which he had
ever visited, and all beyond was an unknown region. But the scenery, as he went onward, was similar in character. The mountains
were higher and more abrupt, the river more rapid
and foamy, and the patches of grass more scanty
—that was all the difference. It was the Arctic
summer, and the night brought no darkness; yet
he knew when the time for rest came, by watching
the direction of the light on the black mountains
above. When the sheep lay down, he sought a
sheltered place under a rock, and slept also.

Next day, the country grew wilder and more
forbidding. Sometimes there was hardly a blade
of grass to be seen for miles, and he drove the
sheep at full speed, running and shouting behind
them, in his eagerness to reach the distant

pasture which Eyvindur had described. In the afternoon, the valley appeared to come suddenly to an end. The river rushed out of a deep cleft between the rocks, only a few feet wide, on the right hand; in front there was a long stony slope, reaching so high that the clouds brushed along its summit. In the bottom there was some little grass, but hardly enough to feed the flock for two days.

Jon was disappointed, but not much discouraged. He tethered Thor securely to a rock, knowing that the other sheep would remain near him, and set out to climb the slope. Up and up he toiled; the air grew sharp and cold; there was snow and ice in the shaded hollows on either side, and the dark, strange scenery of Iceland grew broader below him. Finally, he gained the top; and now, for the first time, felt that he had found a new world. In front, toward the north, there was a plain stretching as far as he could see; on the right and left there were groups of dark, frightful, inaccessible mountains, between the sharp peaks of which sheets of blue ice plunged downward like cataracts, only they were silent and motionless. The valley behind him was a mere cleft in the stony, lifeless world; his sheep were little white dots, no bigger, apparently, than flowers of life-everlasting. He could only guess, beyond the dim ranges in the distance, where his father's dwelling lay; and, for a single moment, the thought came into his mind and made him tremble—should he ever see it again?

The pasture, he reflected, must be sought for in the direction from which the river came. Following the ridge to the eastward, it was not long before he saw a deep basin, a mile in diameter, opening among the hills. The bottom was quite green, and there was a sparkle here and there, where the river wound its way through it. This was surely the place, and Jon felt proud that he had so readily discovered it. There were several glens which furnished easy paths down from the table-land, and he had no difficulty, the next morning, in leading his flock over the great ridge. In fact, they skipped up the rocks as if they knew what was coming, and did not wait for Jon to show them the way into the valley.

The first thing the boy did, after satisfying himself that the sheep were not likely to stray

away from such excellent pasturage, was to seek
for a cave or hollow among the rocks, where he
could find shelter from storms. There were several such places; he selected the most convenient, which had a natural shelf for his store of
provisions, and, having dried enough grass to
make a warm, soft bed, he found himself very
comfortably established. For three or four days,
he was too busy to feel his loneliness. The valley belonged to nobody; so he considered it his
own property, and called it Gudridsdale, after his
sister. Then, in order to determine the bound-
aries of this new estate, he climbed the heights
in all directions, and fixed the forms of every crag
and hollow firmly in his memory. He was not
without the secret hope that he might come upon
some strange and remarkable object,—a deserted
house, a high tree, or a hot fountain shooting up
jets like the Great Geyser,—but there was nothing.
Only the black and stony wilderness near at hand,
and a multitude of snowy peaks in the distance.

Thus ten days passed. The grass was not
yet exhausted, the sheep grew fat and lazy, and
Jon had so thoroughly explored the neighborhood

of the valley that he could have found his way in
the dark. He knew that there were only barren,
uninhabitable regions to the right and left; but
the great, bare table-land stretching to the northward was a continual temptation, for there were
human settlements beyond. As he wandered
farther and farther in that direction, he found it
harder to return; there was always a ridge in
advance, the appearance of a mountain pass,
the sparkle of a little lake—some promise of
something to be seen by going just a little beyond
his turning-point. He was so careful to notice
every slight feature of the scenery,—a jutting
rock here, a crevice there,—in case mist or rain
should overtake him on the way, that the whole
region soon became strangely familiar.

Jon's desire to explore the road leading to the
northward grew so strong, that he at last yielded
to it. But first he made every arrangement for
the safety of the sheep during his absence. He
secured the ram Thor by a long tether and an
abundance of cut grass; concealed the rest of his
diminishing supply of provisions; climbed the
nearest heights and overlooked the country on all

sides without discovering a sign of life, and then, after a rest which was more like a waking dream than a slumber, began his strange and solitary journey.

The sun had just become visible again, low in the north-east, when he reached the level of the table-land. There were few clouds in the sky, and but little wind blowing; yet a singular brownish haze filled the air, and spots of strong light soon appeared on either side of the sun. Jon had often seen these "mock suns" before; they are frequent in northern latitudes, and are supposed to denote a change in the weather. The phenomenon, and the feeling of heaviness in the air, led him to study the landmarks very keenly and cautiously as he advanced. In two or three hours he had passed the limits of his former excursions; and now, if a storm should arise, his very life might depend on his being able to find the way back.

During the day, however, there was no change in the weather. The lonely, rugged mountains, the dark little lakes of melted snow lying at their feet, the stony plain, with its great irregular fissures where the lava had cracked in cooling,—all

these features of the great central desert of Iceland lay hard and clear before his eyes.   Like all
persons who are obliged to measure time without
a watch or clock, he had a very correct sense of
the hours of the day, and of the distances he
walked from point to point.   Where there was no
large or striking object near at hand, he took the
trouble to arrange several stones in a line pointing to the next landmark behind him, as a guide
in case of fog.

It was an exciting, a wonderful day in his life,
and Jon never forgot it.   He never once thought
of the certain danger which he incurred.   Instead
of fear, he was full of a joyous, inspiring courage ;
he sang and shouted aloud, as some new peak or
ridge of hills arose far in front, or some other
peak, already familiar, went out of sight far behind
him.   He scarcely paused to eat or rest, until
nearly twelve hours had passed, and he had
walked fully thirty miles.   By that time the sun
was low in the west, and barely visible through
the gathering haze.   The wind moaned around
the rocks with a dreary, melancholy sound, and
only the cry of a wild swan was heard in the dis-

tance. To the north the mountains seemed higher, but they were divided by deep gaps which indicated the commencement of valleys. There, perhaps, there might be running streams, pastures, and the dwellings of men!

Jon had intended to return to his flock on the morrow, but now the temptation to press onward for another day became very great. His limbs, however, young and strong as they were, needed some rest; and he speedily decided what to do next. A lighter streak in the rocky floor of the plain led his eye toward a low, broken peak—in reality, the crater of a small extinct volcano—some five miles off, and lying to the right of what he imagined to be the true course. On the left there were other peaks, but immediately in front nothing which would serve as a landmark. The crater, therefore, besides offering him some shelter in its crevices, was decidedly the best starting-point, either for going on or returning. The lighter color of the rock came from some different mixture in the lava of an old eruption, and could easily be traced throughout the whole intervening distance. He followed it rapidly, now that the

3*

bearings were laid down, and reached the ruins of the volcano a little after sunset.

There was no better bed to be found than the bottom of a narrow cleft, where the winds, after blowing for many centuries, had deposited a thin layer of sand. Before he lay down, Jon arranged a line of stones, pointing toward the light streak across the plain, and another line giving the direction of the valleys to the northward.   To the latter he added two short, slanting lines at the end, forming a figure like an arrow-head, and then, highly satisfied with his ingenuity, lay down in the crevice to sleep.   But his brain was so excited that for a long time he could do nothing else than go over, in memory, the day's journey.   The wind seemed to be rising, for it whistled like a tremendous fife through the rocky crevice; father and mother and Gudrid seemed to be far, far away, in a different land; he wondered at last, whether he was the same Jon Sigurdson who drove the flock of sheep up the valley of the Thiörvà—and then, all at once, he stopped wondering and thinking, for he was too soundly asleep to dream even of a roasted potato.

I V.

OW much time passed in the sleep he could never exactly learn ; probably six to seven hours. He was aroused by what seemed to be icy-cold rats' feet scampering over his face, and as he started and brushed them away with his hand, his ears became alive to a terrible, roaring sound. He started up, alarmed, at first bewildered, then suddenly wide awake. The cold feet upon his face were little threads of water trickling from above ; the fearful roaring came from a storm—a hurricane of mixed rain, wind, cloud, and snow. It was day, yet still darker than the Arctic summer night, so dense and black was the tempest. When Jon crept out of the crevice, he was nearly thrown down by the force of the wind. The first thing he did was to seek the two lines of stones he had arranged for his guidance. They had not been blown away,

as he feared; and the sight of the arrow-head
made his heart leap with gratitude to the Provi-
dence which had led him, for without that sign he
would have been bewildered, at the very start.
Returning to the cleft, which gave a partial shelter, he ate the greater part of his remaining store
of food, fastening his thick coat tightly around his
breast and throat, and set out on the desperate
homeward journey, carefully following the lighter
streak of rock across the plain.

He had not gone more than a hundred yards
when he fancied he heard a sharp, hammering
sound through the roar of the tempest, and
paused to listen. The sound came rapidly
nearer; it was certainly the hoofs of many horses.
Nothing could be seen; the noise came from the
west, passed in front of Jon, and began to die
away to the eastward. His blood grew chilled
for a moment. It was all so sudden and strange
and ghostly, that he knew not what to think; and
he was about to push forward and get out of the
region where such things happened, when he
heard, very faintly, the cry which the Icelanders
use in driving their baggage-ponies. Then he

JON'S MEETING WITH THE HORSEMEN.

remembered the deep gorge he had seen to the eastward, before reaching the crater; the invisible travellers were riding toward it, probably lost, and unaware of their danger.

This thought passed through Jon's mind like a flash of lightning; he shouted with all the strength of his voice.

He waited, but there was no answer. Then he shouted again, while the wind seemed to tear the sound from his lips and fling it away—but on the course the hoofs had taken.

This time a cry came in return; it seemed far off, because the storm beat against the sound. Jon shouted a third time, and the answer was now more distinct. Presently he distinguished words:

"Come here to us!"

"I cannot!" he cried.

In a few minutes more he heard the hoofs returning, and then the forms of ponies became visible through the driving snow-clouds. They halted, forming a semicircle in front of him; and then one of three dim, spectral riders leaning forward again called: "Come here!"

"I cannot!" Jon answered again.

Thereupon, another of the horsemen rode close to him, and stared down upon him. He said something which Jon understood to be : " Erik, it is a little boy!"—but he was not quite sure, for the man's way of talking was strange. He put the words in the wrong places, and pronounced them curiously.

The man who had first spoken jumped off his horse. Holding the bridle, he came forward and said, in good, plain Icelandic :

"Why could n't you come when I called you ? "

" I am keeping the road back," replied Jon; " if I move, I might lose it."

" Then why did you call us ? "

" I was afraid you had lost your way, and might get into the chasm ; the storm is so bad you could not see it."

" What's that ? " exclaimed the first who had spoken.

Jon described the situation as well as he could, and the stranger at last said, in his queer, broken speech : " Lost way—we ; can guide—you—know how ? "

The storm raged so furiously that it was with great difficulty that Jon heard the words at all; but he thought he understood the meaning. So he looked the man in the face, and nodded, silently.

"Erik—pony!" cried the latter.

Erik caught one of the loose ponies, drew it forward, and said to Jon:

"Now mount and show us the way!"

"I cannot!" Jon repeated. "I will guide you; I was on my way already, but I must walk back just as I came, so as to find the places and know the distances."

"Sir," said Erik, turning to the other traveller, "we must let him have his will. It is our only chance of safety. The boy is strong and fearless, and we can surely follow where he was willing to go alone."

"Take the lead, boy!" the other said; "more quick, more money!"

Jon walked rapidly in advance, keeping his eyes on the lighter colored streak in the plain. He saw nothing, but every little sign and landmark was fixed so clearly in his mind that he did not feel the least fear or confusion. He could hardly see, in fact, the foremost of the ponies behind him, but he caught now and then a word, as the men talked with each other. They had come from the northern shore of the island; they were lost, they were chilled, weary; their ponies were growing weak from hunger and exposure to the terrible weather; and they followed him, not so much because they trusted his guidance, as because there was really nothing else left for them to do.

In an hour and a half they reached the first landmark; and when the men saw Jon examining the line of stones he had laid, and then striking boldly off through the whirling clouds, they asked no questions, but urged their ponies after him. Thus several hours went by. Point after point was discovered, although no object could be seen until it was reached; but Jon's strength, which had been kept up by his pride and his anxiety, at last began to fail. The poor boy had been so long exposed to the wind, snow, and icy rain, that his teeth chattered in his head, and his legs trembled as he walked. About noon, fortunately, there was a lull in the storm; the rain slackened, and the clouds lifted themselves so that one might see for a mile or more. He caught sight of the rocky corner for which he was steering, stopped, and pointed toward one of the loose ponies.

Erik jumped from the saddle, and threw his arms. around Jon, whose senses were fast vanishing. He felt that something was put to his lips, that he was swallowing fire, and that his icy hands were wrapped in a soft, delicious warmth. In a minute he found that Erik had thrust them under his jacket, while the other two were bending over him with anxious faces. The stranger who spoke so curiously held a cake to his mouth, saying: "Eat—eat!" It was wonderful how his strength came back!

Very soon he was able to mount the pony and take the lead. Sometimes the clouds fell dense and dark around them; but when they lifted only for a second, it was enough for Jon. Men and beasts suffered alike, and at last Erik said:

"Unless we get out of the desert in three hours, we must all perish!"

Jon's face brightened. "In three hours," he

exclaimed, "there will be pasturage, and water, and shelter."

He was already approaching the region which he knew thoroughly, and there was scarcely a chance of losing the way. They had more than one furious gust to encounter—more than one moment when the famished and exhausted ponies halted and refused to move; but toward evening the last ridge was reached, and they saw below them, under a dark roof of clouds, the green valley-basin, the gleam of the river, and the scattered white specks of the grazing sheep.

V.

THE ram Thor bleated loudly when he saw his master. Jon was almost too weary to move hand or foot, but he first visited every sheep, and examined his rough home under the rock, and his few remaining provisions, before he sat down to rest. By this time, the happy ponies were appeasing their hunger, Erik and his fellow-guide had pitched a white tent, and there was a fire kindled. The owner of the tent said something which Jon could not hear, but Erik presently shouted:

"The English gentleman asks you to come and take supper with us!"

Jon obeyed, even more from curiosity than hunger. The stranger had a bright, friendly face, and stretched out his hand as the boy entered the tent. "Good guide—eat!" was all that he was able to say in Icelandic, but the tone of his voice

meant a great deal more. There was a lamp
hung to the tent-pole, an india-rubber blanket
spread on the ground, and cups and plates, which
shone like silver, in readiness for the meal.   Jon
was amazed to see Erik boiling three or four tin
boxes in the kettle of water ; but when they had
been opened, and the contents poured into basins,
such a fragrant steam rose as he had never
smelled in his life.   There was pea-soup, and
Irish stew, and minced collops, and beef,—and
tea, with no limit to the lumps of sugar,—and
sweet biscuits, and currant jelly !   Never had he
sat down to such a rich, such a wonderful ban-
quet.   He was almost afraid to take enough of
the dishes, but the English traveller filled his
plate as fast as it was emptied, patted him on the
back, and repeated the words : " Good guide—
eat ! "   Then he lighted a cigar, while Erik and
the other Icelander pulled out their horns of snuff,
threw back their heads, and each poured nearly
a teaspoonful into his nostrils.   They offered the
snuff to Jon, but he refused both that and a cigar.
He was warm and comfortable, to the ends of his
toes, and his eyelids began to fall, in spite of all

efforts to hold them up, after so much fatigue and
exposure as he had endured.

In fact, his senses left him suddenly, although
he seemed to be aware that somebody lifted and
laid him down again—that something soft came
under his head, and something warm over his
body—that he was safe, and sheltered and happy.

When he awoke it was bright day. He
started up, striking his head against a white wet
canvas, and sat a moment, bewildered, trying to
recall what had happened. He could scarcely
believe that he had slept all night in a tent, beside the friendly Englishman; but he heard Erik
talking outside, and the crackling of a fire, and the
shouting of some one at a distance. The sky was
clear and blue; the sheep and ponies were nib-
bling sociably together, and the Englishman,
standing on a rock beside the river, was calling
attention to a big salmon which he had just
caught. Gudridsdale, just then, seemed the
brightest and liveliest place in Iceland.

Jon knew that he had probably saved the
party from death; but he thought nothing of that,
for he had saved himself along with them. He

was simply proud and overjoyed at the chance of
seeing something new—of meeting with a real
Englishman, and eating (as he supposed) the
foreign, English food.   He felt no longer shy,
since he had slept a whole night beside the traveller.   The two Icelandic guides were already
like old friends; even the pony he had ridden
seemed to recognize him.   His father had told
him that Latin was the language by which all
educated men were able to communicate their
ideas; so as the Englishman came up, with his
salmon for their breakfast, he said, in Latin :

"To-day is better than yesterday, sir."

The traveller laughed, shook hands heartily,
and answered in Latin, with—to Jon's great surprise—two wrong cases in the nouns :

"Both days are better for you than for me.   I
have learned less at Oxford."

But the Latin and Icelandic together were a
great help to conversation, and almost before he
knew what he was doing, Jon had told Mr. Lorne
—so the traveller was named—all the simple
story of his life, even his claim to the little valley-
basin wherein they were encamped, and the giv-

ing it his sister's name. Mr. Lorne had crossed from the little town of Akureyri, on the northern shore of Iceland, and was bound down the valley of Thiörva to the Geysers, thence to Hekla, and finally to Rejkiavik, where he intended to embark for England. As Jon's time of absence had expired, his provisions being nearly consumed, and as it was also necessary to rest a day for the sake of the traveller's ponies, it was arranged so that all should return in company to Sigurd's farm.

That last day in Gudricsdale was the most delightful of all. They feasted sumptuously on the traveller's stores, and when night came, the dried grass from Jon's hollow under the rock was spread within the tent, making a soft and pleasant bed for the whole party.

Mounted on one of the ponies, Jon led the way up the long ravine, cheerily singing as he drove the full-fed sheep before him. They reached the level of the desert table-land, and he gave one more glance at the black, scattered mountains to the northward, where he had passed two such adventurous days. In spite of all that he had seen and learned in that time, he felt a

4

little sad that he had not succeeded in crossing the wilderness. When they reached the point where their way descended by a long deep slope to the valley of the Thiörvǎ, he turned for yet another farewell view. Far off, between him and the nearest peak, there seemed to be a moving speck. He pointed it out to Erik, who, after gazing steadily a moment, said : " It is a man on horseback."

" Perhaps another lost traveller ! " exclaimed Mr. Lorne; "let us wait for him."

It was quite safe to let the sheep and loose ponies take their way in advance; for they saw the pasture below them. In a quarter of an hour the man and horse could be clearly distinguished. The former had evidently seen them also, for he approached much more rapidly than at first.

All at once Jon cried out: " It is our pony, Heimdal! It must be my father ! "

He sprang from the saddle as he spoke, and ran toward the strange horseman. The latter presently galloped up, dismounted, walked a few steps, and sat down upon a stone. But Jon's arms were around him, and as they kissed each other, the father burst into tears.

"I thought thou wert lost, my boy," was all he could say.

"But here I am, father!" Jon proudly exclaimed.

"And the sheep?"

"Fat and sound, every one of them."

Sigurd rose and mounted his horse, and as they all descended the slope together Jon and Erik told him all that had happened. Mr. Lorne, to whom the occurrence was explained, shook hands with him, and, pointing to Jon, said in his broken way: "Good son—little man!" Whereupon they all laughed, and Jon could not help noticing the proud and happy expression of his father's face.

On the afternoon of the second day they reached Sigurd's farm-house; but the mother and Gudrid, who had kept up an anxious look-out, met them nearly a mile away. After the first joyous embrace of welcome, Sigurd whispered a few words to his wife, and she hastened back, to put the guest-room in order. Mr. Lorne found it so pleasant to get under a roof again, that he ordered another halt of two days before going on to the

Geysers and Hekla.   No beverage ever tasted so sweet to him as the great bowl of milk which Gudrid brought, as soon as he had taken his seat, and the radishes from the garden seemed a great deal better than the little jar of orange marmalade which he insisted on giving in exchange for them.

"Oh, is it indeed orange?" cried Gudrid. "Jon, Jon, now we shall know what the taste is!"   .

Their mother gave them a spoonful a-piece, and Mr. Lorne smiled as he saw their wondering, delighted faces.

"Does it really grow on a tree?—and how high is the tree?—and what does it look like? like a birch?—or a potato-plant?" Jon asked, in his eagerness, without waiting for the answers. It was very difficult for him to imagine what he had never seen, even in pictures, or anything resembling it.   Mr. Lorne tried to explain how different are the productions of nature in warmer climates, and the children listened as if they could never hear enough of the wonderful story. At last Jon said, in his firm quiet way: "Some day I'll go there!"

"You will, my boy," Mr. Lorne replied; "you have strength and courage to carry out your will."

Jon never imagined that he had more strength or courage than any other boy, but he knew that the Englishman meant to praise him, so he shook hands as he had been taught to do on receiving a gift.

The two days went by only too quickly. The guest furnished food both for himself and the family, for he shot a score of plovers and caught half a dozen fine salmon. He was so frank and cheerful that they soon became accustomed to his presence, and were heartily sorry when Erik and the other Icelandic guide went out to drive the ponies together, and load them for the journey. Mr. Lorne called Sigurd and Jon into the guest-room, untied a buckskin pouch, and counted out fifty silver rix-dollars upon the table. "For my little guide!" he said, putting his hand on Jon's thick curls. Father and son, in their astonishment, uttered a cry at the same time, and neither knew what to say. But, brokenly as Mr. Lorne talked, they understood him when he said that Jon had probably saved his life, that he was a brave boy and would make a good, brave man, and that if the father did not need the money for his farm expenses, he should apply it to his son's education.

The tears were running down Sigurd's cheeks. He took the Englishman's hand, gave it a powerful grip, and simply said: "It shall be used for his benefit."

Jon was so strongly moved that, without stopping to think, he did the one thing which his heart suggested. He walked up to Mr. Lorne, threw his arms around his neck, and kissed him very tenderly.

"All is ready, sir!" cried Erik, at the door. The last packages were carried out and tied upon the baggage-ponies, farewells were said once more, and the little caravan took its way down the valley. The family stood in front of the house, and watched until the ponies turned around the first cape of the hills and disappeared; then they could only sit down and talk of all the unexpected things that had happened. There was no work done upon the farm that day.

V I.

THE unusual warmth of the summer, which was so injurious to the pastures lying near the southern coast, brought fortune to Sigurd's farm. The price of wool was much higher than usual, and owing to Jon's excursion into the mountains, the sheep were in the best possible condition. They had never raised such a crop of potatoes, nor such firm, thick-headed cabbages, and by great care and industry a sufficient supply of hay had been secured for the winter.

"I am afraid something will happen to us," said Sigurd one day to his wife; "the good luck comes too fast."

"Don't say that!" she exclaimed. "If we were to lose Jon——"

"Jon!" interrupted Sigurd. "Oh, no; look at his eyes, his breast, his arms and legs—there

are a great many years of life in them! He
ought to have a chance at the school in Rejkiavik, but we can hardly do without him this year."

"Perhaps brother Magnus would take him,"
she said.

"Not while I live," Sigurd replied, as he left
the room, while his wife turned with a sigh to
her household duties. Her family, and especially
her elder brother, Magnus, who was a man of
wealth and influence, had bitterly opposed her
marriage with Sigurd, on account of the latter's
poverty, and she had seen none of them since
she came to live on the lonely farm. Through
great industry and frugality, they had gradually
prospered; and now she began to long for a
reconciliation, chiefly for her husband's and children's sake. It would be much better for Jon if
he could find a home in his uncle's house, when
they were able to send him to school.

So, when they next rode over to Kyrkedal on
a Sabbath day in the late autumn, she took with
her a letter to Magnus, which she had written
without her husband's knowledge, for she wished
to save him the pain of the slight, in case her

brother should refuse to answer or should answer in an unfriendly way. It was a pleasant day for all of them, for Mr. Lorne had stopped a night at Kyrkedal, and Erik had told the people the story of Jon's piloting them through the wilderness; so the pastor, after service, came up at once to them and patted Jon on the head, saying: "*Bene fecisti, fili!*" And the other boys, forgetting their usual shyness, crowded around and said: "Tell us all about it!" Everything was as wonderful to them, as it still seemed to Jon in his memory, and when each one said: "If I had gone there I should have done the same thing!" Jon wondered that he and the boys should ever have felt so awkward and bashful when they came together. Now it was all changed; they talked and joked like old companions, and cordially promised to visit each other during the winter, if their parents were willing.

On the way home Sigurd found that he had dropped his whip, and sent Jon back to look for it, leaving his wife and Gudrid to ride onward up the valley. Jon rode at least half a mile before he found it, and then came galloping back, cracking

4*

it joyously.   But Sigurd's face was graver and wearier than usual.

"Ride a little while with me," he said; "I want to ask thee something."   Then, as Jon rode beside him in the narrow tracks which the ponies' hoofs had cut through the turf, he added: "The boys at Kyrkedal seemed to make much of thee; I hope thy head is not turned by what they said."

"Oh, father!" Jon cried; "they were so kind, so friendly!"

"I don't doubt it," his father answered. "Thou hast done well, my son, and I see that thou art older than thy years.   But suppose there were a heavier task in store for thee,—suppose that I should be called away,—couldst thou do a man's part, and care properly for thy mother and thy little sister?"

Jon's eyes filled with tears, and he knew not what to say.

"Answer me!" Sigurd commanded.

"I never thought of that," Jon answered, in a trembling voice; "but if I were to do my best, would not God help me?"

"He would!" Sigurd exclaimed, with energy.

" All strength comes from Him, and all fortune.
Enough—I can trust thee, my son; ride on to
Gudrid, and tell her not to twist herself in the
saddle, looking back!"

Sigurd attended to his farm for several days
longer, but in a silent, dreamy way, as if his mind
were busy with other thoughts. His wife was so
anxiously waiting the result of her letter to Magnus, that she paid less attention to his condition
than she otherwise would have done.

But one evening, on returning from the stables,
he passed by the table where their frugal supper
was waiting, entered the bedroom, and sank down,
saying:

" All my strength has left me; I feel as if I
should never rise again."

They then saw that he had been attacked by
a dangerous fever, for his head was hot, his eyes
glassy, and he began to talk in a wild, incoherent
way. They could only do what the neighbors
were accustomed to do in similar cases,—which
really was worse than doing nothing at all would
have been. Jon was dispatched next morning, on
the best pony, to summon the physician from

Skalholt ; but, even with the best luck, three
days must elapse before the latter could arrive.
The good pastor of Kyrkedal came the next day
and bled Sigurd, which gave him a little tempo-
rary quiet, while it reduced his vital force. The
physician was absent, visiting some farms to the
eastward,—in fact, it was a full week before he
made his appearance. During this time Sigurd
wasted away, his fits of delirium became more frequent, and the chances of his recovery grew less
and less. Jon recalled, now, his father's last conversation, and it gave him both fear and comfort.
He prayed, with all the fervor of his boyish nature,
that his father's life might be spared; yet he
determined to do his whole duty, if the prayer
should not be granted.

VII.

T the end of two weeks, Sigurd's wife received a letter from her brother, and it was better than she had dared to hope. Magnus wrote that his wife was dead, his son was a student in Copenhagen, and he was all alone in the big house at Rejkiavik. He was ready to give Jon a home, even to take herself and her husband, provided the latter could sell his farm to good advantage and find some employment which would add to his means. " He must neither live an idle life, nor depend on my help," Magnus said; and his sister felt that he was right, although he told the truth in rather a hard, unfriendly way.

She read the letter to Sigurd the next morning, as he was lying very weak and quiet, but in his right mind. His eyes slowly brightened, and he murmured, at last, with difficulty:

"Sell the farm to Thorsten, for his eldest son, and go to Magnus. Jon will take my place."

Jon, who had entered the room in time to hear these words, sat down on the bed and held his father's hand in both his own. The latter smiled faintly, opened his lips to speak again, and then a sudden quivering passed over his face, and he lay strangely still. It was a long time before the widow and children could believe he was dead. They said to each other, over and over again, amid their tears: "He was happy; the trouble for our sakes was taken away from his heart;"—and Jon thought to himself: "If I do my best, as I promised, he will be still happier in heaven."

When Sigurd's death was known, the neighbors came and helped them until the funeral was over, and the sad little household resumed, as far as possible, its former way of life. Thorsten, a rich farmer of Kyrkedal, whose son was to be married in the spring, came, a few weeks later, to make an offer for the farm. No doubt he hoped to get it at a low price; for money has a greater value in Iceland, where there is so little of it. But the widow said at once: "I shall make no bargain unless Jon agrees with me;" and then Jon spoke up, looking a great deal more like a full-grown honest man than he supposed:

"We only want the fair value of the farm, neighbor Thorsten. We want it because we need it, and everybody will say it is just and right that we should have it. If we cannot get that, I shall try to go on and do my father's work. I am only a boy now, but I shall get bigger and stronger every year."

"Thy father could not have spoken better words," said Thorsten.

He made what he considered a fair offer, and it was very nearly as much as Jon and his mother had reckoned upon; the latter, however, insisted on waiting until she had consulted with her brother Magnus.

Not many days after that, Magnus himself arrived at the farm. He was a tall man, with dark hair, large grey eyes, a thin, hard mouth, and an important, commanding air. It was a little hard for Jon to say "uncle" to this man, whom he had never seen, and of whom he had heard so little. Magnus, although stern, was not unfriendly, and when he had heard of all that had been said and done, he nodded his head and said:

"Very prudent; very well, so far!"

It was, perhaps, as well that the final settlement of affairs was left to Uncle Magnus, for he not only obtained an honest price for the farm, but sold the ponies, cows, and sheep to much better advantage than the family could have done. He had them driven to Kyrkedal, and sent messengers to Skalholt and Myrdal, and even to Thingvalla, so that quite a number of farmers came together, and they had dinner in the church. Some of the women and children also came, to say "good-bye" to the family; but when the former whispered to Jon: "You'll come back to us some day, as a pastor or a *skald*" (author), Magnus frowned and shook his head.

"The boy is in a fair way to make an honest, sensible man," he said. "Don't you spoil him with your nonsense!"

When they all set out together for Rejkiavik, Jon reproached himself for feeling so light-hearted, while his mother and Gudrid wept for miles of the way. He was going to see a real town, to enter school, to begin a new and wonderful life ; and just beyond Kyrkedal there came the first strange sight. They rode over the grassy plain toward the Geysers, the white steam of which they had often seen in the distance ; but now, as they drew near a grey cone, which rose at the foot of the hill on the west, a violent thumping began in the earth under their feet. " He is going to spout ! " cried the guide, and he had hardly spoken when the basin in the top of the cone boiled over furiously, throwing huge volumes of steam into the air. Then there was a sudden, terrible jar, and a pillar of water, six feet in diameter, shot up to the height of nearly a hundred feet, sparkling like liquid gold in the low, pale sunshine. It rose again and again, until the subterranean force was exhausted ; then the water fell back into the basin with a dull sound, and all was over.

They could think or talk of nothing else for a time, and when they once more looked about them the landscape had changed. All was new to the children, and only dimly remembered by their mother. The days were very short and dark,

for winter was fast coming on; it was often difficult to make the distance from one farm-house to
another, and they twice slept in the little churches,
which are always hospitably opened for travellers,
because there are no inns in Iceland.   After leaving the valley, they had a bitterly cold and stormy
journey over a high field of lava, where little piles
of stones, a few yards apart, are erected to guide
the traveller.   Beyond   this,   they   crossed   the
Raven's Cleft, a deep narrow chasm, with a natural bridge in one place, where the rocks have fallen
together from either side; then, at the bottom of
the last slope of the lava-plains, they entered the
Thingvalla Forest.

Jon was a little disappointed; still he had
never seen anything like it.   There were willow
and birch bushes, three or four feet high, growing
here and there out of the cracks among the rocks.
He could look over the tops of them from his
pony, as he rode along, and the largest trunk was
only big enough to make a club.   But there is no
other "forest" in Iceland; and the people must
have something to represent a forest, or they
would have no use for the word!

It was fast growing dark when they reached Thingvalla, and the great shattered walls of rock which inclose the valley appeared much loftier than by day. On the right, a glimmering waterfall plunged from the top of the cliff, and its roar filled the air. Magnus pointed out, on the left, the famous " Hill of the Law," where for nearly nine hundred years, the people of Iceland had assembled together to discuss their political matters. Jon knew all about the spot, from the many historical legends and poems he had read, and there was scarcely another place in the whole world which he could have had greater interest in seeing. The next morning, when it was barely light enough to travel, they rode up a kind of rocky ladder, through a great fissure called the *Almannagjá*, or "People's Chasm," and then pushed on more rapidly across the barren table-land. It was still forty miles to Rejkiavik,—a good two days' journey at that season,—and the snows, which already covered the mountains, were beginning to fall on the lower country.

On the afternoon of the second day, after they had crossed the Salmon River, Magnus said:

"In an hour we shall see the town!"

But the first thing that came in sight was only a stone tower, or beacon, which the students had built upon a hill.

"Is that a town?" asked Gudrid; whereupon the others laughed heartily.

Jon discreetly kept silent, and waited until they had reached the foot of the beacon, when—all at once—Rejkiavik lay below them. Its two or three hundred houses stretched for half a mile over a belt of land between the sea and a large lake. There was the prison, built all of cut stone; the old wooden cathedral, with its square spire; the large snow-white governor's house, and the long row of stores and warehouses, fronting the harbor —all visible at once! To a boy who had never before seen a comfortable dwelling, nor more than five houses near together, the little town was a grand, magnificent capital. Each house they passed was a new surprise to him; the doors, windows, chimneys and roofs were all so different, so large and fine. And there were more people in the streets than he had ever before seen together.

At last Magnus stopped before one of the

handsomest dwellings, and helped his sister down from her pony. The door opened, and an old servant came forth. Jon and Gudrid, hand in hand, followed them into a room which seemed to them larger and handsomer than the church at Kyrkedal, with still other rooms opening out of it, with wonderful chairs, and pictures, and carpets upon which they were afraid to walk. This was their new home.

EVEN before their arrival, Jon discovered that his Uncle Magnus was a man who said little, but took good notice of what others did. The way to gain his favor, therefore, was to accept and discharge the duties of the new life as they should arise. Having adopted the resolution to do this, it was surprising how soon those duties became familiar and easy. He entered the school, where he was by no means the lowest or least promising scholar, assisted his mother and Gudrid wherever it was possible, and was so careful a messenger that Magnus by degrees intrusted him with matters of some importance. The household, in a little while, became well-ordered and harmonious, and although it lacked the freedom and home-like feeling of the lonely farm on the Thiörvǎ, all were contented and happy.

Jon had a great deal to learn, but his eagerness helped him. His memory was naturally
excellent, and he had been obliged to exercise it
so constantly—having so few books, and those
mostly his own written copies—that he was able
to repeat, correctly, large portions of the native
sagas, or poetical histories. He was so well advanced in Latin that the continuance of the study
became simply a delight; he learned Danish,
almost, without an effort, from his uncle's commer-
cial partner and the Danish clerk in the warehouse ; and he took up the study of English with
a zeal which was heightened by his memories of
Mr. Lorne.

We cannot follow him, step by step, during
this period, although many things in his life
might instruct and encourage other earnest,
struggling boys. It is enough to say that he was
always patient and cheerful, always grateful for
his opportunity of education, and never neglect-
ful of his proper duties to his uncle, mother, and
sister. Sometimes, it is true, he was called upon
to give up hours of sport, days of recreation,
desires which were right in themselves but could

not be gratified,—and it might have gone harder
with him to do so, if he had not constantly
thought: "How would my father have acted
in such a case?" And had he not promised
to take the place of his father?

So three years passed away. Jon was eigh-
teen, and had his full stature. He was strong
and healthy, and almost handsome; and he had
seen so much of the many strangers who every
summer come to Rejkiavik,—French fishermen,
Spanish and German sailors, English travellers,
and Danish traders,—that all his old shyness had
disappeared. He was able to look any man in
the eyes, and ask or answer a question.

It was the beginning of summer, and the
school had just closed. Jon had been assisting
the Danish clerk in the warehouse; but toward
noon, when they had an idle hour, a sailor
announced that there was a new arrival in the
harbor; so he walked down the beach of sharp
lava-sand to the wooden jetty where strangers
landed. A little distance off shore a yacht was
moored; the English flag was flying at the stern,
and a boat was already pulling toward the land-

The Halt on the Journey.

ing-place. Jon rubbed his eyes, to be sure that he saw clearly; but no! the figure remained the same; and now, as the stranger leaped ashore, he could no longer contain himself. He rushed across the beach, threw his arms around the man, and cried out: "Lorne! Lorne!"

The latter was too astonished to recognize him immediately.

"Don't you know me?" Jon asked; and then, half laughing, half crying, said in Latin: "To-day is better than yesterday."

"Why, can this be my little guide?" exclaimed Mr. Lorne. "But to be sure it is! there are no such wise eyes in so young a head anywhere else in the world."

Before night the traveller was installed in the guest-room in Uncle Magnus's house; and then they truly found that he had not forgotten them. After supper he opened a box, and out there came a silver watch for Jon; a necklace, that could not be told from real pearls, for Gudrid; and what a shawl for the mother! Even Uncle Magnus was touched, for he brought up a very old, dusty bottle of Portugal wine, which he had

never been known to do before, except one day
when the Governor came to see him.

"And now," said Mr. Lorne, when he was a
little tired of being thanked so much, "I want
something in return.   I am going, by way of the
Broad Fiord, to the northern shore of Iceland,
and back through the desert; and I shall not feel
safe unless Jon goes with me."

"Oh!" cried Jon.

"I am not afraid this time," said Gudrid.

Magnus looked at his sister, and then nodded.
"Take the boy!" he said.   "He can get back
before school commences again; and we are
as ready to trust him with you, as you are to trust
yourself with him."

What a journey that was!   They had plenty
of ponies, and a tent, and provisions in tin cans.
Sometimes it rained or snowed, and they were
wet and chilly enough at the end of the day, but
then the sun shone again, and the black mountains became purple and violet, and their snows
and ice-fields sparkled in the blue of the air.
They saw many a wild and desolate landscape,
but also many a soft green plain and hay-meadow

along the inlets of the northern shore ; and in the
little town of Akureyri Jon at last found a tree—
the only tree in Iceland ! It is a mountain-ash,
about twenty feet high, and the people are so
proud of it that every autumn they wrap the trunk
and boughs, and even the smallest twigs, in woolen
cloth, lest the severity of the winter should kill it.

They visited the *Myvatn* (Mosquito Lake) in
the north-eastern part of the island, saw the volcanoes which in 1875 occasioned such terrible
devastation, and then crossed the great central
desert to the valley of the Thiörva. So it happened that Jon saw Gudridsdale again, but under
pleasanter aspects than before, for it was a calm,
sunny day when they reached the edge of the
table-land and descended into the lovely green
valley. It gave him a feeling of pain to find
strangers in his father's house, and perhaps Mr.
Lorne suspected this, for he did not stop at the
farm, but pushed on to Kyrkedal, where the good
old pastor entertained them both as welcome
guests. At the end of six weeks they were back
in Rejkiavik, hale and ruddy after their rough
journey, and closer friends than ever.

Each brought back his own gain—Mr. Lorne was able to speak Icelandic tolerably well, and Jon was quite proficient in English. The former had made the trip to Iceland especially to collect old historical legends and acquire new information concerning them. To his great surprise, he found Jon so familiar with the subject, that, during the journey, he conceived the idea of taking him to Scotland for a year, as an assistant in his studies; but he said nothing of this until after their return. Then, first, he proposed the plan to Magnus and Jon's mother, and prudently gave them time to consider it. It was hard for both to consent, but the advantages were too evident to be rejected. To Jon, when he heard it, it seemed simply impossible; yet the preparations went on,—his mother and Gudrid wept as they helped, Uncle Magnus looked grave,—and at last the morning came when he had to say farewell.

The yacht had favorable winds at first. They ran along the southern shore to Ingolf's Head, saw the high, inaccessible summits of the Skaptar Jökull fade behind them, and then Iceland dropped below the sea. A misty gale began to blow from the south-west, forcing them to pass the Faroe Islands on the east, and afterward the Shetland Isles; but, after nearly coming in sight of Norway, the wind changed to the opposite quarter, and the yacht spread her sails directly for Leith. One night, when Jon awoke in his berth, he missed the usual sound of waves against the vessel's side and the cries of the sailors on deck—everything seemed strangely quiet; but he was too good a sleeper to puzzle his head about it, so merely turned over on his pillow. When he arose the quiet was still there. He dressed in haste and went on deck. The yacht lay at anchor in front of buildings larger than a hundred Rejkiaviks put together.

"This is Leith," said Mr. Lorne, coming up to him.

"Leith?" Jon exclaimed; "it seems like Rome or Jerusalem! Those must be the king's palaces."

"No, my boy," Mr. Lorne answered, "they are only warehouses."

"But what are those queer green hills behind the houses? They are so steep and round that I don't see how anybody could climb up."

" Hills ? " exclaimed Mr. Lorne. "Oh, I see now ! Why, Jon, those are trees."

Jon was silent. He dared not doubt his friend's word, but he could not yet wholly believe it. When they had landed, and he saw the great trunks, the spreading boughs, and the millions of green leaves, such a feeling of awe and admiration came over him that he began to tremble. A wind was blowing, and the long, flexible boughs of the elms swayed up and down.

" Oh, Mr. Lorne ! " he cried. " See ! they are praying ! Let us wait awhile ; they are saying something—I hear their voices. Is it English?— can you understand it ? "

Mr. Lorne took him by the hand, and said : " It is praise, not prayer. They speak the same language all over the world, but no one can understand all they say."

There is one rough little cart in Rejkiavik, and this is the only vehicle in Iceland. What, then, must have been Jon's feelings when he saw hundreds of elegant carriages dashing to and fro, and great wagons drawn by giant horses ? When they got into a cab, it seemed to him like sitting on a moving throne. He had read and heard of all these things, and thought he had a clear idea of what they were; but he was not prepared for the reality. He was so excited, as they drove up the street to Edinburgh, that Mr. Lorne, sitting beside him, could feel the beating of his heart. The new wonders never ceased: there was an apple-tree, with fruit; rose-bushes in bloom; whole beds of geraniums in the little gardens; windows filled with fruit, or brilliant silks, or silver-ware; towers that seemed to touch the clouds, and endless multitudes of people! As they reached the hotel, all he could say, in a faltering voice, was: "Poor old Iceland!"

The next day they took the train for Lanark, in the neighborhood of which Mr. Lorne had an estate. When Jon saw the bare, heather-covered mountains, and the swift brooks that came leaping down their glens, he laughed and said:

"Oh, you have a little of Iceland even here! If there were trees along the Thiörvä, it would look like yonder valley."

"I have some moorland of my own," Mr.

Lorne remarked; "and if you ever get to be homesick, I'll send you out upon it to recover."

But when Jon reached the house, and was so cordially welcomed by Mrs. Lorne, and saw the park and gardens where he hoped to become familiar with trees and flowers, he thought there would be as much likelihood of being homesick in heaven as in such a place.

Everything he saw tempted him to visit and examine it. During the first few days he could scarcely sit still in the library and take part in Mr. Lorne's studies. But his strong sense of duty, his long habits of patience and self-denial, soon made the task easy, and even enabled him to take a few more hours daily for his own improvement. His delight in all strange and beautiful natural objects was greatly prolonged by this course. He enjoyed everything far more than if he had rapidly exhausted its novelty. Mr. Lorne saw this quality of Jon's nature with great satisfaction, and was very ready to give advice and information which he knew would be earnestly heeded.

It was a very happy year; but I do not believe that it was the happiest of Jon's life. Having learned to overcome the restlessness and im-
patience which are natural to boyhood, he laid
the basis for greater content in life as a man.
When he returned to Rejkiavik, in his twentieth
year, with a hundred pounds in his pocket and
a rich store of knowledge in his head, all other
tasks seemed easy. It was a great triumph for his
mother, and especially for Gudrid, now a bright,
blooming maiden of sixteen. Uncle Magnus
brought up another dusty bottle to welcome him,
although there were only six more left; and all the
neighbors came around in the evening. Even the
Governor stopped and shook hands, the next day,
when Jon met him in the street. His mother,
who was with him, said, after the Governor had
passed : " I hope thy father sees thee now." The
same thought was in Jon's heart.

And now, as he is no longer a boy, we must
say good-bye to him. We have no fears for his
future life ; he will always be brave, and manly,
and truthful. But, if some of my readers are still
curious to know more of him, I may add that he

is a very successful teacher in the school at Rejkiavik ; that he hopes to visit Mr. Lorne, in Scotland, very soon ; and I should not be in the least
surprised if he were to join good old Dr. Hjalta-
lin, and pay a visit to the United States.

STORY IV.

THE TWO HERD-BOYS.

WHEN I was in Germany, several years ago, I spent a few weeks of the summertime in a small town among the Thuringian Mountains. This is a range on the borders of Saxony, something like our Green Mountains in height and form, but much darker in color, on account of the thick forests of fir which cover them. I had visited this region several times before, and knew not only the roads, but most of the foot-paths, and had made some acquaintance with the people: so I felt quite at home among them, and was fond of taking long walks up to the ruins of castles on the peaks, or down into the wild, rocky dells between them.

The people are mostly poor, and very laborious; yet all their labor barely produces enough to keep them from want. There is not much farming land, as you may suppose. The men cut wood, the women spin flax and bleach linen, and the children gather berries, tend cattle on the high mountain pastures, or act as guides to the summer travellers. A great many find employment in the manufacture of toys, of which there are several establishments in this region, producing annually many thousands of crying and speaking dolls, bleating lambs, barking dogs, and roaring lions.

Behind the town where I lived, there was a spur of the mountains, crowned by the walls of a

castle built by one of the Dukes who ruled over
that part of Saxony eight or nine hundred years
ago. Beyond this ruin, the mountain rose more
gradually, until it reached the highest ridge, about
three miles distant. In many places the forest
had been cut away, leaving open tracts where the
sweet mountain grass grew thick and strong, and
where there were always masses of heather, hare-
bells, foxgloves, and wild pinks. Every morning
all the cattle of the town were driven up to these
pastures, each animal with a bell hanging to its
neck, and the sound of so many hundred bells
tinkling all at once made a chime which could be
heard at a long distance.

One of my favorite walks was to mount to the
ruined castle, and pass beyond it to the flowery
pasture-slopes, from which I had a wide view of
the level country to the north, and the mountain-
ridges on both sides. Here, it was very pleasant
to sit on a rock, in the sunny afternoon, and listen
to the continual sound of bells which filled the air.
Sometimes one of the herd-boys would sing, or
shout to the others across the intervening glens,
while the village girls, with baskets of bark, hunt-

ed for berries along the edges of the forests. Although so high on the mountain, the landscape was never lonely.

One day, during my ramble, I came upon two smaller herds of cattle, each tended by a single boy. They were near each other, but not on the same pasture, for there was a deep hollow, or dell, between. Nevertheless they could plainly see each other, and even talk whenever they liked, by shouting a little. As I came out of a thicket upon the clearing, on one side of the hollow, the herd-boy tending the cattle nearest to me was sitting among the grass, and singing with all his might the German song, commencing,

> " Tra, ri, ro !
> The summer's here, I know !"

His back was towards me, but I noticed that his elbows were moving very rapidly. Curious to learn what he was doing, I slipped quietly around some bushes to a point where I could see him distinctly, and found that he was knitting a woolen stocking. Presently he lifted his head, looked across to the opposite pasture, and cried out, " Hans! the cows!"

THE TWO HERD-BOYS. 113

I looked also, and saw another boy of about the same age start up and run after his cattle, the last one of which was entering the forests. Then the boy near me gave a glance at his own cattle, which were quietly grazing on the slope, a little below him, and went on with his knitting. As I approached, he heard my steps and turned towards me, a little startled at first; but he was probably accustomed to seeing strangers, for I soon prevailed upon him to tell me his name and age. He was called Otto, and was twelve years old; his father was a wood-cutter, and his mother spun and bleached linen.

"And how much," I asked him, "do you get for taking care of the cattle?"

"I am to have five thalers," (about four dollars,) he answered, "for the whole summer: but it doesn't go to me, it's for father. But then I make a good many groschen by knitting, and *that's* for my winter clothes. Last year I could buy a coat, and this year I want to get enough for trousers and new shoes. Since the cattle know me so well, I have only to talk and they mind me; and that, you see, gives me plenty of time to knit."

"I see," I said; "it's a very good arrangement. I suppose the cattle over on the other
pasture don't know their boy? He has not got
them all out of the woods yet."

"Yes, they know him," said Otto, "and that's
the reason they slip away. But the cattle mind
some persons better than others; I've seen that
much."

Here he stopped talking, and commenced
knitting again. I watched him awhile, as he
rapidly and evenly rattled off the stitches. He
evidently wanted to make the most of his time.
Then I again looked across the hollow, where
Hans—the other boy—had at last collected his
cows. He stood on the top of a rock, flinging
stones down the steep slope. When he had no
more, he stuck his hands in his pockets and
whistled loudly, to draw Otto's attention; but the
latter pretended not to hear. Then I left them;
for the shadow of the mountain behind me was
beginning to creep up the other side of the
valley.

A few days afterwards I went up to the pasture again, and came, by chance, to the head of

the little dell dividing the two herds. I had been wandering in the fir-forest, and reached the place unexpectedly. There was a pleasant view from the spot, and I seated myself in the shade, to rest and enjoy it. The first object which attracted my attention was Otto, knitting as usual, beside his herd of cows. Then I turned to the other side to discover what Hans was doing. His cattle, this time, were not straying; but neither did he appear to be minding them in the least. He was walking backwards and forwards on the mountain-side, with his eyes fixed upon the ground. Some-times, where the top of a rock projected from the soil, he would lean over it, and look along it from one end to the other, as if he were trying to meas-ure its size; then he would walk on, pull a blue flower, and then a yellow one, look at them sharply, and throw them away. "What is he after?" I said to myself, "has he lost something, and is trying to find it? or are his thoughts so busy with something else that he does n't really know what he is about."

I watched him for nearly half an hour, at the end of which time he seemed to get tired, for he

gave up looking about and sat down in the grass.
The cattle were no doubt acquainted with his
ways—(it is astonishing how much intelligence
they have!)—and they immediately began to
move towards the forest, and would soon have
wandered away, if I had not headed them off and
driven them back. Then I followed them, much
to the surprise of Hans, who had been aroused by
the noise of their bells as they ran from me.

"You don't keep a very good watch, my
boy!" I said. '

As he made no answer, I asked, " Have you
lost anything ? "

" No," he then said.

"What have you been hunting so long ? "

He looked confused, turned away his head, and
muttered, " Nothing."

This made me sure he had been hunting
something, and I felt a little curiosity to know
what it was. But although I asked him again,
and offered to help him hunt it, he would tell me
nothing. He had a restless and rather unhappy
look, quite different from the bright, cheerful eyes
and pleasant countenance of Otto.

His father, he said, worked in a mill below the town, and got good wages; so he was allowed half the pay for tending the cattle during the summer.

"What will you do with the money?" I asked.

"O, I'll soon spend it," he said. "I could spend a hundred times that much, if I had it."

"Indeed!" I exclaimed. "No doubt it's all the better that you have n't it."

He did not seem to like this remark, and was afterwards disinclined to talk; so I left him and went over to Otto, who was as busy and cheerful as ever.

"Otto," said I, "do you know what Hans is hunting, all over the pasture? Has he lost anything?"

"No," Otto answered; "he has not lost anything, and I don't believe he will find anything, either. Because, even if it is all true, they say you never come across it when you look for it, but it just shows itself all at once, when you're not expecting."

"What is it, then?" I asked.

Otto looked at me a moment, and seemed to

hesitate. He appeared also to be a little surprised : but probably he reflected that I was a
stranger, and could not be expected to know
everything ; for he finally asked, " Don't you
know, sir, what the shepherd found, somewhere
about here, a great many hundred years ago ? "

" No," I answered.

" Not the key-flower ? "

Then I *did* know what he meant, and understood the whole matter in a moment. But I wanted to know what Otto had heard of the story, and
therefore said to him, " I wish you would tell me."

" Well," he began, " some say it was true, and
some that it wasn't. At any rate, it was a long,
long while ago, and there's no telling how much
to believe. My grandmother told *me ;* but then
she did n't know the man : she only heard about
him from her grandmother. He was a shepherd,
and used to tend his sheep on the mountain,—or
may be it was cows, I'm not sure,—in some place
where there were a great many kobolds and fairies.
And so it went on, from year to year. He was a
poor man, but very cheerful, and always singing
and making merry ; but sometimes he would wish

to have a little more money, so that he need not
be obliged to go up to the pastures in the cold,
foggy weather. That wasn't much wonder, sir,
for it's cold enough up here, some days.

"It was in summer, and the flowers were all
in blossom, and he was walking along after his
sheep when all at once he saw a wonderful sky-
blue flower of a kind he had never seen before in
all his life. Some people say it was sky-blue, and
some that it was golden-yellow: I don't know
which is right. Well, however it was, there was
the wonderful flower, as large as your hand, growing in the grass. The shepherd stooped down
and broke the stem; but just as he was lifting up
the flower to examine it, he saw that there was a
door in the side of the mountain. Now he had
been over the ground a hundred times before,
and had never seen anything of the kind. Yet it
was a real door, and it was open, and there was a
passage into the earth. He looked into it for a
long time, and at last plucked up heart and in he
went. After forty or fifty steps, he found himself
in a large hall, full of chests of gold and diamonds. There was an old kobold, with a white

beard, sitting in a chair beside a large table in the middle of the hall.   The shepherd was at first frightened, but the kobold looked at him with a friendly face, and said, ' Take what you want, and don't forget the best ! '

"So the shepherd laid the flower on the table, and went to work and filled his pockets with the gold and diamonds.   When he had as much as he could carry, the kobold said again, ' Don't forget the best ! '   ' That I won't,' the shepherd thought to himself, and took more gold and the biggest diamonds he could find, and filled his hat, so that he could scarcely stagger under the load. He was leaving the hall, when the kobold cried out, ' Don't forget the best ! '   But he couldn't carry any more, and went on, never minding. When he reached the door in the mountain-side, he heard the voice again, for the last time, ' Don't forget the best ! '

"The next minute he was out on the pasture. When he looked around, the door had disappeared : his pockets and hat grew light all at once, and instead of gold and diamonds he found nothing but dry leaves and pebbles.   He was as

poor as ever, and all because he had forgotten the
best. Now, sir, do you know what the best was?
Why, it was the flower, which he had left on the
table in the kobold's hall. *That* was the key-
flower. When you find it and pull it, the door is
opened to all the treasures under ground. If the
shepherd had kept it, the gold and diamonds
would have stayed so; and, besides, the door
would have been always opened to him, and he
could then help himself whenever he wanted."

Otto had told the story very correctly, just as
I had heard it told by some of the people before.
" Did you ever look for the key-flower ? " I asked
him.

He grew a little red in the face, then laughed,
and answered: " O, that was the first summer I
tended the cattle, and I soon got tired of it. But
I guess the flower does n't grow any more, now."

" How long has Hans been looking for it?"

" He looks every day," said Otto, "when he
gets tired doing nothing. But I shouldn't wonder
if he was thinking about it all the time, or he'd
look after his cattle better than he does."

As I walked down the mountain that after-
6

noon I thought a great deal about these two herd-
boys and the story of the key-flower.   Up to this
time the story had only seemed to me to be a
curious and beautiful fairy-tale; but now I began
to think it might mean something more.   Here
was Hans, neglecting his cows, and making himself restless and unhappy, in the hope of some day
finding the key-flower; while Otto, who remembered that it can't be found by hunting for it, was
attentive to his task, always earning a little, and
always contented.

Therefore, the next time I walked up to the
pastures, I went straight to Hans.   "Have you
found the key-flower yet?" I asked.

There was a curious expression upon his face.
He appeared to be partly ashamed of what he
must now and then have suspected to be a folly,
and partly anxious to know if I could tell him
where the flower grew.

"See here, Hans," said I, seating myself upon
a rock.   "Don't you know that those who hunt
for it never find it.   Of course you have not found
it, and you never will, in this way.   But even if
you should, you are so anxious for the gold and

diamonds that you would be sure to forget the best, just as the shepherd did, and would find nothing but leaves and pebbles in your pockets."

"O, no!" he exclaimed; "that's just what I wouldn't do."

"Why, don't you forget your work every day?" I asked. "You are forgetting the best all the time,—I mean the best that you have at present. Now I believe there is a key-flower growing on these very mountains; and, what is more, Otto has found it!"

He looked at me in astonishment.

"Don't you see," I continued, "how happy and contented he is all the day long? He does not work as hard at his knitting as you do in hunting for the flower; and although you get half your summer's wages, and he nothing, he will be richer than you in the fall. He will have a small piece of gold, and it won't change into a leaf. Besides, when a boy is contented and happy he has gold and diamonds. Would you rather be rich and miserable, or poor and happy?"

This was a subject upon which Hans had evidently not reflected. He looked puzzled. He was so accustomed to think that money embraced everything else that was desirable, that he could not imagine it possible for a rich man to be miserable. But I told him of some rich men whom I knew, and of others of whom I had heard, and at last bade him think of the prosperous brewer in the town below, who had had so much trouble in his family, and who walked the streets with his head hanging down.

I saw that Hans was not a bad boy : he was simply restless, impatient, and perhaps a little inclined to envy those in better circumstances. This lonely life on the mountains was not good for a boy of his nature, and I knew it would be difficult for him to change his habits of thinking and wishing. But, after a long talk, he promised me he would try, and that was as much as I expected.

Now, you may want to know whether he *did* try ; and I am sorry that I cannot tell you. I left the place soon afterwards, and have never been there since. Let us all hope, however, that he found the real key-flower.

STORY V.

THE YOUNG SERF.

I.

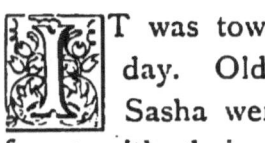T was towards the close of a September day. Old Gregor and his grandson Sasha were returning home through the forest with their bundles of wood, the old man stooping low under the weight of the heavier sticks he carried, while the boy dragged his great bunch of twigs and splints by a rope drawn over his shoulder. Where the trees grew thick, the air was already quite gloomy, but in the open spaces they could see the sky and tell how near it was to sunset.

Both were silent, for they were tired, and it is not easy to talk and carry a heavy load at the same time. But presently something grey appeared through the trees, at the foot of a low hill; it was the rock where they always rested on the way home. Old Gregor laid down his bundle there, and wiped his face on the sleeve of his brown jacket, but Sasha sprang upon the rock and began to balance himself upon one foot, as was his habit whenever he tried to think about anything.

"Grandfather," he said, at last, "why should all the forest belong to the Baron, and none of it to you?"

Gregor looked at him sharply for a moment, before he answered.

"It was his father's and his grandfather's: it has been the property of the family for many a hundred years, and we have never had any."

"I know that," said Sasha. "But why did it come so *first?*"

Gregor shook his head. "You might as well ask how the world was made." Then, seeing that the boy looked troubled, he added in a kinder tone: "what put such a thought in your head?"

"Why, the forest itself!" Sasha cried. "The Baron lets us have the top branches and little twigs, but he always takes the logs and sells them for money. I know all the trees, and he does n't; I can find my way in the woods anywhere, and there's many a tree that would say to me, if it could talk: 'I'd rather belong to you, Sasha, because I know you.'"

"Aye, and the moon would say the same to you, boy, and the sun and stars, maybe. You might as well want to own them,—and *you* don't even belong to yourself?"

Gregor's words seemed harsh and fierce, but his voice was very sad. Sasha looked at him and knew not what to say, but he felt that his heart was beating violently. All at once he heard a rustling among the dead leaves, and a sound like steps approaching. The old man took hold of his grandson's arm and made a sign to him to be silent. The sound came nearer, and nearer, and presently they could distinguish some dusky object moving towards them through the trees.

"Is it a robber?" whispered Sasha.

"It is not a man, unless he uses his knees for hind-feet. I see his head; it is a bear. Keep quiet, boy! make no noise: take this tough stick, but hold it at your side, as I do with mine. Look him in the face, if he comes close; and if I tell you to strike, hit him on the end of the nose!"

It was, indeed, a full-grown bear, marching slowly on his great flat feet. He was not more than thirty yards distant, when he saw them, and stopped. Both kept their eyes fixed upon his head, but did not move. Then he came a few paces nearer, and Sasha tried hard not to show that he was trembling inwardly, more from excitement than fear. The bear gazed steadily at them for what seemed a long time: there was an expression of anger, but also of stupid bewilderment, in his eyes. Finally he gave a sniff and a grunt, tossed up his nose, and slowly walked on, stopping once or twice to turn and look back, before he disappeared from view. Sasha lifted his stick and shook it towards him; he felt that he should never again be much afraid of bears.

"Now, boy," said Gregor, "you have learned how to face danger. I have been as near to a loaded cannon as to that bear, and the wind of the ball threw me on my face; but I was up the next minute, and then the gunner went down! Our colonel saw it, and I remember what he said—ay, every word! He would have kept his promise, but we carried him from the field next day, and that was the end of the matter. It was in France."

"Grandfather," Sasha suddenly asked, "are there forests in France?—and do they belong to the Barons?"

"Pick up your fagot, boy, and come along! It will be dark before we get to the village, and the potatoes are cooked by this time."

The mention of the potatoes revived all Sasha's forgotten hunger, and he obeyed in silence. After walking for a mile as rapidly as their loads would permit, they issued from the forest, and saw the wooden houses of the village on a green knoll, in the last gleams of sunset. The church, with its three little copper-covered domes, stood on the highest point; next to it the priest's house and garden; then began the broad street, lined with square log-cabins and adjoining stables, sloping down to a large pond, at the foot of which was a mill. Beyond the water there was a great stretch of grazing meadow, then long, rolling fields of rye and barley, extending to the woods which bounded the view in every direction. The village was situated within a few miles of the

6*

great main highway running from Warsaw to
Moscow, and the waters of the pond fed the
stream which flowed into one of the branches of
the river Dnieper.

The whole region, including the village and
nearly all the people in it, belonged to the estate
of Baron Popoff, the roofs of whose residence
were just visible to the southward, on a hill overlooking the road to Moscow. The former castle
had been entirely destroyed during the retreat of
Napoleon's army, and the Baron's grandfather
suffered so many losses at the time that he was
only able to build a large and very plain modern
house; but the people always called it "the Castle," or "the Palace," just as before. Although
the Baron sold every year great quantities of tim-
ber, grain, hemp and wool from his estates, he
always seemed to be in want of money. The
servants who went with him every winter to St.
Petersburg were very discreet, and said little
about their master's habits of life; but the people
understood, somehow, that he often lost large
sums by gambling. This gave them a good deal
of uneasiness, for if he should be obliged to part

with the estate, they would all be transferred, with it, to a new owner—and this might be one who had other estates in other parts of Russia, to which he could send them if he was so minded.

At the time of which I am writing, twenty-two millions of the Russian people were *serfs*. Their labor, even their property, belonged to the owner of the land upon which they lived. The latter had not the power to sell them to another, as was formerly the case with slaves in the South, but he could remove them from one estate to another if he had several. Baron Popoff was a haughty and indifferent master, but not a cruel one; the people of the village had belonged to his family for several generations, and were accustomed to their condition. At least, they saw no way of changing it, except by a change of masters, which was more likely to be a misfortune than a benefit.

It was nearly dark when old Gregor and Sasha threw down their loads, and entered the house. The supper was already waiting, for Sasha's sister, little Minka, had been up to the church door to see whether they were coming. In one corner of the room a tiny lamp was burn-

ing before a picture of the Virgin Mary and Child
Jesus, all covered with gilded brass except the
hands and faces, which were nearly black, partly
from the smoke, and partly because the common
Russian people imagine that the Hebrews were a
very dark-skinned race.   Sasha's father, Ivan, had
also lighted a long pine-splint, and the room
looked very cheerful.   The boiled potatoes were
smoking in a great wooden bowl, beside which
stood a dish of salt, another of melted fat, and a
loaf of black bread.   They had neither plates,
knives nor forks; only some coarse wooden
spoons, and all ate out of the bowl, after the salt
had been sprinkled and the fat poured over the
potatoes.   For drink there was an earthen pitcher
of *quass*, a kind of thin and rather sour beer.

Old Gregor sat on one side of the table, and
his son Ivan with Anna, his wife, opposite.
There were five children, the oldest being Alexander (whom we know by his nickname " Sasha,"
which is the Russian for " Aleck " or " Sandy "),
then Minka, Peter, Waska and Sergius.   Sasha
was about thirteen years old, rather small for his
age, and hardly to be called a handsome boy.

Only there was something very pleasant in his large grey eyes, and his long, thick flaxen hair shone almost like silver when the sun fell upon it. However, he never thought about his looks. When he went to the village bath-house, on a Saturday evening, to take his steam-bath with the rest, the men would sometimes say, after examining his joints and muscles: "You are going to be strong, Sasha!"—and that was as much as he cared to know about himself.

The boy was burning with desire to tell the adventure with the bear, but he did not like to speak before his grandfather, and there was something in the latter's eye which made him feel that he was watching him. Gregor first lighted his pipe, and then, in the coolest possible manner— as if it were something that happened every day —related the story. "Pity I hadn't your gun with me, Ivan," he said at the close: "what with the meat, the fat and the skin, we should have had thirty roubles."

The children were quite noisy with excitement. Little Peter said: "What for did you let him go, Sasha? *I'd* have killed him and carried

him home!"   Then all laughed so heartily that
Peter began to cry and was soon packed into a box in
the corner, where he slept with Waska and Sergius.

"Take the gun with you to-morrow, father,"
said Ivan.

"It's too much, with my load of wood," Gregor answered; "the old hunting-knife is all I
want.   Sasha will stand by me with a club; he'll
not be afraid, the next time."

Sasha was about to exclaim: "I was n't afraid
the first time!" but before he spoke, it flashed
across his mind that he *did* tremble a little—just
a very little.

By this time it was dark outside.   Two pine-
splints had burned out, one after the other, and
only the little lamp before the shrine enabled
them dimly to see each other.   The older people
went to bed in their narrow rooms, which were
hardly better than closets; and Sasha, spreading
a coarse sack of straw on the floor, lay down,
covered himself with his sheep-skin coat, and in
five minutes was so sound asleep that he might
have been dragged about by the heels without
being awakened.

II.

The next day, in the forest, old Gregor worked more rapidly than usual. He spoke very little, in spite of Sasha's eagerness to talk, and kept the boy so busy that all the wood was gathered together and the bundles made up, two or three hours before the usual time.

They were in a partially cleared spot, near the top of some rising ground. The old man looked at the sky, nodded his head, and said with a satisfied air: "We have plenty of time left for ourselves, Sasha: come with me, and I'll show you something."

He set out in a direction opposite from home, and the boy, who expected nothing less than the finding of another bear, seized a tough, straight club, and followed him. They went for nearly a mile over rolling ground, through the forest, and then descended into a narrow glen, at the foot of which ran a rapid stream. Very soon, rocks began to appear on either side, and the glen became a chasm where there was barely room to walk. It was a cold, gloomy, strange place;

Sasha had never seen anything like it. He felt a singular creeping of the flesh, but not for the world would he have turned back.

The path ceased, and there was a waterfall in front, filling up the whole chasm. Gregor pulled off his boots and stepped into the stream, which reached nearly to his knees: he gave his hand to Sasha, who could hardly have walked alone against the force of the current. They reached the foot of the fall, the spray of which was whirled into their faces. Then Gregor turned suddenly to the left, passed through the thin edge of the falling water, and Sasha, pulled after him, found himself in a low, arched vault of rock, into which the light shone down from another opening. They crawled upwards on hands and feet, and came out into a great circular hole, like a kettle, through the middle of which ran the stream. There was no other way of getting into it, for the rocks leaned inward as they rose, making the bottom considerably broader than the top.

On one side, under the middle of the rocky arch, stood a square black stone, about five feet high, with a circle of seven smaller stones, resem-

bling seats, around it. Sasha was dumb with surprise, at finding himself in such a wonderful spot.

But old Gregor made the sign of the cross,
and muttered something which seemed to be a
prayer. Then he went to the black stone, and
put his hand upon it.

"Sasha," he said, "this is one of the places
where the old Russian people came, many thousand years ago, before ever the name of Christ
was heard of. They were dreadful heathen in
those days, and this was what they had in the
place of a church. A black stone had to be the
altar, because they had a black god, who was
never satisfied unless they fed him with human
blood.

"Where is he now?" Sasha asked.

"They say he turned into an evil spirit, and is
hiding somewhere in the wilderness; but I don't
know whether it's true. His name was Perun.
Most men do not dare to say it, but I have the
courage, because I've been a soldier and have an
honest conscience. Are you afraid to stand
here?"

"Not if you are not, grandfather," said Sasha.

"If your heart were bad and false, you might well be afraid. Come here to me."

Sasha obeyed. The old man opened the boy's coarse shirt and laid his hand upon his heart; then he made him do the same to himself, so that the heart of each beat directly against the hand of the other.

"Now, boy," he then said, "I am going to trust you, and if you say a word you do not mean, or think otherwise than you speak, I shall feel it in the motion of your heart. Do you know the difference between a serf and a free man? Would you rather live like your father, without anything he can call his own, or like the Baron, with houses and forests that nobody could take away from you—unless it might be the Emperor?"

Sasha's heart gave a great thump, before he opened his mouth. The old man smiled, and he said to himself: "I was right." Then he continued: "I should be a free man now, if our colonel had lived. Your father had not wit and courage enough to try, but *you* can do it, Sasha, if you think of nothing else and work for nothing else. I will help you all I can ; but you must begin at once. Will you ? "

" Yes ! yes ! " cried Sasha, eagerly.

" Promise me that you will say nothing to any living soul ; that you will obey me and remember all I say to you while I live, and be none the less faithful to the purpose when I am dead ! "

Sasha promised everything, at once. After a moment's silence, Gregor took his hand from the boy's breast, and said : " Yes, you truly mean it. The old people used to say that if anybody broke a promise made before this stone, the black heathen god would have power over him."

" Perhaps the bear was the black god," Sasha suggested.

" Perhaps he was. Look him in the face, as you did yesterday, remember your promise, and he can't harm you."

As they walked slowly back through the forest, Gregor began to talk, and the boy kept close beside him, listening eagerly to every word.

" The first thing," he said, " is to get knowledge. You must learn, somehow, to read and write, and count figures. I must tell you all I know, about everything in the world, but that's very little ; and it's so mixed up in my head, that I don't rightly know where to begin.   It's a bless-ing that I've not forgotten much ; what I picked up I held on to, and now I see the reason why. There's nothing you can't use, if you wait long enough."

" Tell me about France ! " Sasha cried.

"France and Germany too ! I was two or three years, off and on, in those foreign parts, and I could talk smartly in the speech of both—*Al-lez ! Sortez ! Donnez moi du vin !* "

Gregor stopped and straightened his bent back ; his eyes flashed, and he laughed long and heartily.

"*Allez ! Sortez ! Donnez moi du vin !* " re-peated Sasha.

Gregor caught up the boy in his arms, and kissed him.   " The very thing ! " he cried : " I'll teach you both tongues,—and all about the strange habits of the people, and their houses and churches, and which way the battle went, and what queer harness they have on their horses, and a talking bird I once saw, and a man that kept a bottle full of lightning in his room—"

So his tongue ran on. It was a great delight to him to recall his memories of more than thirty years, and he was constantly surprised to find how many little things that seemed forgotten came back to his mind. Sasha's breath came quick, as he listened; his whole body felt warm and nimble, and it suddenly seemed to him possible to learn anything and everything. Before reaching home, he had fixed twenty or thirty French words in his memory. There they were, hard and tight; he knew he should never forget them.

From that day began a new life for both. Old Gregor's method of instruction would simply have confused a pupil less ignorant and less eager to be taught; but Sasha was so sure that knowledge would in some way help him to become a free man, that he seized upon everything he heard. In a few months he knew as much German and French as his grandfather, and when they were alone they always spoke, as much as possible, in one or the other language. But the boy's greatest desire was to learn how to read. During the following winter he made himself use-

ful to the priest in various ways, and finally succeeded in getting from him the letters of the
alphabet and learning how to put them together.
Of course, he could not keep secret all that he
did ; it was enough that no one guessed his
object in doing it.

One day, in the spring, just after the Baron
had returned with his wife from St. Petersburg,
Sasha was sent on an errand to the castle. He
was bare-headed and bare-footed : his shirt and
wide trowsers were very coarse, but clean,
and his hair floated over his shoulders like
a mass of shining silk. When he reached
the castle, the Baron and Baroness, with a
strange lady, were sitting on the balcony. The
latter said, in French: "There's a nice-looking
boy ! "

Sasha was so glad to find that he understood,
and so delighted with the remark, that he looked
up suddenly and blushed.

" I really believe he understands what I said,"
the lady exclaimed.

The Baron laughed. " Do you suppose my
young serfs are educated like princes ? " he

asked. " If he were so intelligent as that, how long could I keep him ? "

Sasha bent down his head, and kicked the loose pebbles with his feet, to hide his excitement. The blood was humming in his ears : the Baron had said the same thing as his grandfather —to get knowledge was the only way to get freedom !

III.

The summer passed away, and the second autumn came. Gregor had told all he knew; told it twice, three times; and Sasha, more eager than ever, began to grow impatient for something more. He had secured a little reading-book, such as is used for children, and studied it until he knew the exact place of every letter in it, but there was none to give the poor boy another volume, or to teach him anything further.

One afternoon, as he was returning alone from a neighboring village by a country-road which branched off from the main highway, he saw three men sitting on the bank, under the edge of a thicket. They were strangers, and they seemed to him to be foreigners. Two were of middle age, with harsh, evil faces: the third was young, and had an anxious, frightened look. They were talking earnestly, but before he could distinguish the words, one of them saw him, made a sign to the others, and then he was very sure that they suddenly changed their language; for it was German he now heard.

He felt proud of his own knowledge, and his first thought was to say "good-day!" in German. Then he remembered his grandfather's command: "Never show your knowledge until there's a good reason for it!" and gave his greeting in Russian. The young man nodded in return; the others took no notice of him. But in passing he understood these sentences:

"He will bring a great deal of money. . . There's no danger—he will be alone. . . . . Grain and hemp both sold to-day . . . . . It will be already dark."

Just beyond the thicket the road made a sharp turn and entered the woods. Sasha never afterwards could quite explain the impulse which led him to dart under the trees as soon as he was out of sight, to get in the rear of the thicket, crawl silently nearer on his hands and knees, and then lie down flat within hearing of the men's voices. For a moment, he was overcome with a horrible fear. They were silent, and his heart beat so loudly that he thought they could no more help noticing it than a blacksmith's hammer.

Presently one of them spoke,—this time in Russian. "There's a hill from which you can see both roads," he said; "but he'll hardly take the highway."

"Are you sure his groom was not in the town?" asked another.

"It's all as I say—rely upon that!" was the answer. "For all his title he's no more than another man, and we are three!"

In talking further, they mentioned the name of the town; it was the place only a few miles distant, where the grain, hemp and other products of the estate were sold to traders—and this was the day of the sale! The plot of the robbers flashed into Sasha's mind; and, if he had had any remaining doubts, they were soon dissipated by his hearing the Baron's name. The latter was to

7

be waylaid—plundered—killed, if he resisted.
Then the oldest of the three men said, as he got
up from the bank where they were sitting,

"We must be on the way. Better be too
early than too late."

"But it's a terrible thing," the youngest remarked.

"You can't turn back now!" the other cried.

Sasha waited until he could no longer hear
their footsteps. Then he started up, and keeping
away from the road they had taken, ran through
the woods and thicket in the direction of the
town. His only thought was, to reach the hill
the robbers had mentioned, from which both
roads could be seen. He knew it well; there
was a bridle-path, shorter than the main highway,
and the Baron would probably take it, as he was
on horseback. The hill divided the two roads;
it was covered with young birch-trees, which grew
very thickly on the summit and almost choked up
the path. But there was a long spur of thicket,
he remembered, running out on the ridge, and
whoever stood at the end of it could almost look
into the town.

Sasha was so excited that he took a track almost as short as a bird flies. He tore through bushes and brambles without thinking of the scratches they gave him; he jumped across gullies and ran at full speed over open fields; he was faint, and bruised, and breathless, but he never paused until the farthest point of the thicket on the hill was reached. It was then about an hour before sunset, and only one or two foot-travellers were to be seen upon the highway. The town was half a mile off, but he could plainly see where the bridle-track issued from a little lane between the houses. Carefully concealing himself under a thick alder-bush, he kept his eyes fixed upon that point.

He was obliged to wait for what seemed a long, long while. The sun was just setting when, finally, a horseman made his appearance, and Sasha knew by the large white horse that it must be the Baron. The rider looked at his watch, and then began to canter along the level towards the hill. There was no time to lose; so, without pausing a moment to think, Sasha sprang out of his hiding-place, and darted down the grassy

slope at full speed, crying "Lord Baron! Lord
Baron!"

The rider, at first, did not seem to heed. He
cantered on, and it required all Sasha's remaining strength to reach the path in advance of
him. Then he dropped upon his knees, lifted up
his hands, and cried once more: "Stop, Lord
Baron!"

The Baron reined up his horse just in time
to avoid trampling on the boy. Sasha sprang to.
his feet, seized the bridle, and gasped: "the
robbers!"

"Who are you?—and what does this mean?"
the Baron asked in a stern voice.

But Sasha was too much in earnest to feel
afraid of the great lord. "I am Sasha, the son of
Ivan, the son of Gregor," he said; and then related, as rapidly as he could, all that he had seen
and heard.

The Baron looked at his pistols. "Ha!" he
cried, "the caps are taken off! You may have
done me good service, boy. Wait here: it's not
enough to escape the rascals; we must capture
them!"

He turned his horse, and galloped back at full speed toward the town. Sasha watched him, thinking only that he was saved, at last. It was growing dark, when the boy's quick ear caught the sound of steps in the opposite direction. He turned and saw the three men approaching rapidly. With a deadly sense of terror he started and ran towards the town.

" Kill the little spy !" shouted, behind him, a voice which he well knew.

Sasha cried aloud for help, as he ran; but no help came. He was already weak and exhausted from the exertion he had made, and he heard the robbers coming nearer and nearer. All at once it seemed to him that his cries were answered; but at the same moment a heavy blow came down upon his head and shoulder. He fell to the ground, and knew no more.

IV.

When Sasha came to his senses, it seemed to him that he must have been dead for a long time. First of all, he had to think who he was; and this was not so easy as you may suppose, for he found himself lying in bed, in a room he had never seen before. It was broad daylight, and the sun shone upon one of his hands, which was so white and thin that it did not seem to belong to him. Then he lifted it, and was amazed to find how little strength there was in his arm. But he brought it to his head, at last,—and there was another surprise. All his long, silken hair was gone! He was so weak and bewildered that he groaned aloud, and the tears ran down his cheeks.

There was a noise in the room, and presently old Gregor bent over the bed.

" Grandad," said the boy—and how feeble his voice sounded !—" am I your Sasha still ? "

The old man, crying for joy, dropped on his knees and said a prayer. " Now you will get well ! " he cried; " but you musn't talk ; the doctor said you were not to talk ! "

" Where am I ? " Sasha asked.

" At the Palace ! And the Baron's own doctor comes every day to see you ; and they let me stay here to nurse you—it will be a week to-morrow ! "

" What's the matter ? "—what has happened ? "

"Don't talk, for the love of Heaven!" said Gregor: "you saved the Baron from being robbed and killed; and the head-robber struck your head and broke your arm; and the Baron and the people came just at the right time; and one of them was shot, and the other two are in jail! O, my boy, remember the altar of the black god, Perun: be obedient to me: shut your eyes and keep quiet!"

But Sasha could not shut his eyes. Little by little his memory came back, and a sense of what he had done filled his mind and made him happy. He felt a dull ache in his left arm, and found that it was so tightly bandaged he could not move it; so he lay quite still, while Gregor sat and watched him with sparkling eyes. After a time the door opened, and a strange gentleman came in; it was the physician. The old man rose and conversed with him in whispers. Then Sasha found that a spoon was held to his lips; he mechanically swallowed something that had a strange, pleasant taste, and almost immediately fell asleep.

In a day or two he was strong enough to sit

up in bed, and was allowed to talk. Then the
Baron and Baroness came, with the lady who was
their guest, to see him. They were all eager to
learn the particulars of the occurrence, especially
how Sasha had discovered the plot of the robbers.
He began at the beginning, and had got as far as
the latter's change of language on seeing him,
when he stopped in great confusion and looked at
his grandfather.

Gregor neither spoke nor moved, but his eyes
seemed to say plainly: "tell everything."

Sasha then related the whole story, to the end.
The Baroness came to the bedside, stooped down,
kissed him, and said: "You have saved your
lord!"

But the other lady, who had been watching
him very curiously, suddenly exclaimed: "Why,
it's the same nice-looking little serf I saw before;
and when I spoke of him in French, he blushed.
I'm sure he understood me! Don't you understand me now, my boy?"

She asked the question in French, and Sasha
answered in the same language: "Yes, madam."

The lady clapped her hands in delight; but

the Baron asked very sternly: "Where did you learn so many languages?"

"From me!" Gregor answered. "The boy likes to know things, and I've always thought—saving your opinion, my good lord—that when God gives any one a strong wish for knowledge, He means it to be answered. So I opened to him all there is in this foolish old head of mine, while we were together in the forest; and it was such a pleasure for him to take that it came to be a pleasure for me to give. You understand, my lady?"

"Yes," said the Baroness, "I understand that without Sasha's knowledge of German, my husband would probably have been murdered."

"That's not so certain," the Baron replied. "But some celebrated man has said: 'All's well that ends well.' The fellow did his duty like a full-grown man, and I'll take care of him."

Therewith they went out of the room, and Sasha immediately asked, in some anxiety: "Grandfather, you meant I should tell?"

"Yes," Gregor answered; "for the youngest robber has already confessed that they spoke in

German, and thought themselves safe, while you
were passing. They are vagabonds from the
borders of Poland, and knew a little of three or
four tongues. It is all right, my boy: the Baron
is satisfied, and means to help you. Your chance
has come sooner than I expected. I must have a
little time to think about it; my head is like
a stiff joint, hard to bend when I want to use it.
It's good-luck to me that you can't get out of bed
for a week to come ! "

He laughed as he left the bedside, and took
his seat on the broad stone bench beside the
stove. Sasha kept silent, for he knew that the
old man's brain was hard at work. He tried to
do a little thinking, himself, but it made him feel
weak and giddy; in fact, the blow upon his head
would have killed a more delicate boy.

His strength came back so rapidly, however,
that in a week he was able to walk out, with his
arm in a sling. He was still pale, and looked so
strange in his short hair, that on his first visit
home his mother burst into tears on seeing him.
Then Minka, Peter, Sergius and Waska lifted up
their voices and cried; and Ivan, who was at first

angry with them, finally cried also, without knowing why he did it. All this made Sasha feel very
uncomfortable, and he was on the point of saying :
" I won't do it again ! " when old Gregor made
silence in the house. He had looked through the
window and seen some of the neighbors coming ;
so the whole family became cheerful again, as
rapidly as they could.

By this time, Gregor had made up his mind.
Sasha knew that he could not change it if he
would, and he was therefore very glad to find how
well his grandfather's notions agreed with his
own. While he was waiting for the Baron to
speak again, he was not losing time ; for the
strange lady who was visiting at the castle took
quite a friendly interest in teaching him French
and German, and giving him Russian books
which were not too difficult to read. He was so
eager to satisfy her, that he really made astonishing progress.

When the robbers were tried before the judge,
he was called upon to give testimony against
them. One of the three having been killed, the
youngest one was not afraid to confess, and his

story and Sasha's agreed perfectly. The boy
described the unwillingness of the former to un-
dertake the crime : even the Baron said a word in
his favor ; and the judge, at last, sentenced him
to be banished to Siberia for only ten years, while
the older robber was sent there for life.

That evening, the Baron asked Sasha :
"Would you like to be one of my house-ser-
vants, boy ? "

Just as his grandfather had advised him,
Sasha answered : "It is not for me to choose, my
lord ; but I think I can serve you much more to
your profit if you will let me try to become a
merchant."

" A merchant ! " the Baron exclaimed.

" Not all at once," said Sasha : "I could be of
use now, as a boy to help carry and sell things,
because I can count, and speak a little in other
tongues. I should make myself so useful to
some merchant that he would give me a chance
to learn the whole business, in time. Then I
should earn much money, and could pay you for
the privilege."

The Baron had often envied noblemen of his

acquaintance, some of whose serfs were rich manufacturers or merchants, and paid them large annual sums for the privilege of living for themselves. Here seemed to be a chance for him to gain something in the same way. The boy spoke so confidently, and looked in his face with such straight-forward eyes, that he felt obliged to consider the proposition seriously.

"How will you get to St. Petersburg?" he asked.

"When you go, my lord," said Sasha, "I could sit on the box, at the coachman's feet. I will help him with the horses, and it shall cost you nothing. When I get there, I know I shall find a place."

The Baron then said: "You may go."

V.

Here, as a boy not yet fifteen, Sasha begins his career as a man. The task he has undertaken demands the industry, the patience and the devotion of his life, but he has been prepared for it by a sound if a somewhat hard experience. I hope the boys who read this feel satisfied, already, that

he is going to succeed; yet I know, also, that
they like to be certain, and to have some little
information as to how it came about.   So I will
let fifteen years pass, and we will now look upon
Sasha, for the last time, as a man of thirty.

He has a store and warehouse on the great
main street of St. Petersburg, which is called
the *Nevsky Prospekt,*—that is the Perspective of
the Neva, because, when you look down it
you see the blue waters of the river Neva at the
end.   Over the door there is a large sign, with
the name : " Alexander Ivanovitch."   [*Ivanovitch*
means " the son of Ivan :" Russian family names
are formed in this manner, and therefore the son
has a different name from the father, unless their
baptismal names are the same.]   He employs a
number of clerks and salesmen, and has a servant
who would go through fire and water to help him.
I must relate how he found this man, and why the
latter is so faithful.

On one of his journeys of business, five years
before, Sasha visited the town of Perm, on the
western side of the Ural Mountains.   It is on the
main highway to Siberia, and criminals are con-

tinually passing, either on the way thither in chains, or returning in rags when their time of banishment has expired. One evening, Sasha found by the roadside, in the outskirts of the town, a miserable looking wretch who seemed to be at the point of death. He felt the man's pulse, lifted up his head and looked in his face, and was startled at recognizing the younger of the three robbers. He had him taken to the inn, tended and restored, and after being convinced of his earnest desire to lead a better life, gave him employment. The robber was not naturally a bad man, but very ignorant and superstitious. It seemed to him both a miracle and a warning that he should have been saved by Sasha, and he fully believed that his soul would be lost if he should ever act dishonestly towards him.

Keeping his heart steadily upon the great purpose of his life, Sasha rose from one step to another until he became an independent and wealthy merchant,—far wealthier, indeed, than the Baron supposed. He paid the latter a handsome annual sum for his time, and sent only small presents of money to his parents, for he knew how

few and simple their needs were.   He felt, a thousand times more keenly than old Gregor, what it
was to be a serf.   The old man was still living,
but very feeble and helpless, and Sasha often
grew wild at the thought that he might die before
knowing freedom.

His plan of action had long been fixed, and
now the hour had come when he determined to
try it.   He had for years kept a strict watch over
the Baron's life in St. Petersburg, knew the
amount of his increasing debts and the embarrass-
ment they occasioned him, and could very nearly
calculate the moment when ruin would come.
He was not disappointed, therefore, at receiving
an urgent summons from his master.

"Sasha," said the latter, laying his hand
upon the serf's shoulder with a familiarity he had
never displayed before, "You are an honest, faithful fellow.   I need a few thousand roubles for a
month or two: can you get the money for
me ? "

"I have heard, my lord," Sasha answered,
"that you are in difficulty.   I knew why you sent
for me; and I come to offer you a way out of all

your troubles. Your debts amount to more than
a hundred thousand roubles : would you like to
be relieved of them ? ".

"Would I not!—but how ? " the Baron cried.

"I will pay them, my lord; but you will do
one thing for me in return."

" You ?—You ? "

" I," Sasha quietly answered : " I will free you,
and you will free me."

"Ha!" the Baron cried, springing to his feet.
His pride was touched. He was fond of boasting
that he, also, had a serf who was a rich merchant,
and the fact had many a time helped his credit
when he wanted to borrow money. Uncon-
sciously, he shook his head.

" You have not the money," he said.

Sasha, who understood what was passing
through the Baron's mind, suffered so much from
his cruel uncertainty that he turned deadly pale.

"I am well known," he answered, "and can
procure the money in an hour. How much is my
serfdom worth to you ? My annual payment is
hardly one-tenth of the usurious interest which
your debt wrings from you : I offer to release you

from all trouble, and thus add not less than eight
thousand roubles a year to your income. And
my freedom, which you can now sell back to me
at such a price, may be mine without buying, in a
few years more ! "

The Emperor, Alexander II., had at that time
just succeeded to the throne, and his intention to
emancipate the serfs was already suspected by the
people. Sasha knew that he was running a great
risk in what he said ; but his clasped hands, his
trembling voice, his eyes filled with tears, affected
the Baron more powerfully than his words.

There was a long silence. The master turned
away to the window, and weighed the offer rapidly in his mind : the serf waited, in breathless
anxiety, in the centre of the room.

Suddenly the Baron turned and struck his
clenched fist on the table. Then he stretched
out his hand, and said : " Alexander Ivanovitch, I
am glad to make your acquaintance as a friend :
I am no longer your master."

Sasha took the hand, kissed it, and his tears
fell fast. "Dear lord Baron !" he cried; "Give
also the freedom of my father and grandfather,

and I will add a payment of five thousand roubles a year, for ten years to come!"

"And your ancestors for five hundred years back," the Baron answered, laughing. "I don't know their names, but they can be all thrown into the deed, in one lump."

Before another day, it was done. Sasha and the living members of his family were free, and his ancestors would also have been free if they had not been dead. With the parchment, signed and sealed, in his pocket, he took a carriage and post-horses and travelled day and night until he reached his native village. No one knew the stranger, in his rich merchant's dress: his father and brothers were in the fields at work, and his mother had stepped out to see a neighbor: old Gregor was alone in the house. He was leaning back, in a rude arm-chair, with a sheep-skin over his knees; his eyes were closed, his mouth slightly open, and his face so haggard and sunken that Sasha thought him dead.

He kneeled down beside the chair, and placed his hand on the old man's heart, to see if it still beat. Presently came a broken voice: "The black god—the truth, my boy!" and Gregor feebly stretched a hand toward Sasha's breast. The latter tore open his dress, and spread the cold, horny fingers over his own heart, the warmth of which seemed to kindle a fresh life in the old man. He at last opened his eyes: "little Sasha," he said; "little Sasha will keep his word."

"I have kept it, grandfather!" Sasha cried.

"It's a man, a brave-looking man," said Gregor; "but he has the boy's voice—and I know the boy's hand is on my heart."

Sasha could no longer restrain himself. "And the boy is a free man, grandfather!" he exclaimed; " we are all free: here is the Baron's deed, which says so, with the seal of the Empire upon it. Look, grandfather!—do you understand, you are free?"

Gregor was lifted to his feet, as if by an unseen hand. At that moment Sasha's parents and brothers entered the house. The old man did not heed their cries of astonishment: clasping the parchment to his breast, he looked upward and exclaimed in a piercing voice: "Free at last,—all free! I'll carry the news to God!" Then with a single gasp he reeled, and, before any one could reach him, fell at full length on the floor, dead.

Putnams' Series of Popular Manuals.

HALF-HOURS WITH THE MICROSCOPE.

By EDWIN LANKESTER, M.D., F.R.S. Illustrated by 250 Drawings from Nature. 12mo, cloth, $1.25.

"This beautiful little volume is a very complete manual for the amateur microscopist. * * * The 'Half-Hours' are filled with clear and agreeable descriptions, whilst eight plates, executed with the most beautiful minuteness and sharpness, exhibit no less than 250 objects with the utmost attainable distinctness."—*Critic.*

HALF-HOURS WITH THE TELESCOPE:

Being a popular Guide to the Use of the Telescope as a means of Amusement and Instruction. Adapted to inexpensive instruments. By R. A. PROCTOR, B.A., F.R.A.S. 12mo, cloth, with illustrations on stone and wood. Price, $1.25.

"It is crammed with starry plates on wood and stone, and among the celestial phenomena described or figured, by far the larger number may be profitably examined with small telescopes."—*Illustrated Times.*

HALF-HOURS WITH THE STARS:

A Plain and Easy Guide to the Knowledge of the Constellations, showing in 12 Maps, the Position of the Principal Star-Groups Night after Night throughout the Year, with introduction and a separate explanation of each Map. True for every Year. By RICHARD A. PROCTOR, B.A., F.R.A.S. Demy 4to. Price, $2.25.

"Nothing so well calculated to give a rapid and thorough knowledge of the position of the stars in the firmament has ever been designed or published hitherto. Mr. Proctor's 'Half-Hours with the Stars' will become a text-book in all schools, and an invaluable aid to all teachers of the young."— *Weekly Times.*

MANUAL OF POPULAR PHYSIOLOGY:

Being an Attempt to Explain the Science of Life in Untechnical Language. By HENRY LAWSON, M.D. 18mo, with 90 Illustrations. Price, $1.25.

Man's Mechanism, Life, Force, Food, Digestion, Respiration, Heat, the Skin, the Kidneys, Nervous System, Organs of Sense, &c., &c., &c.

"Dr Lawson has succeeded in rendering his manual amusing as well as instructive. All the great facts in human physiology are presented to the reader successively; and either for private reading or for classes, this manual will be found well adapted for initiating the uninformed into the mysteries of the structure and function of their own bodies."—*Athenæum.*

WOMAN BEFORE THE LAW.

By JOHN PROFFATT, LL.B., of the New York Bar.

CONTENTS.—I. Former Status of Women. II. Legal Conditions of Marriage. III. Personal Rights and Disabilities of the Wife. IV. Rights of Property, Real and Personal. V. Dower. VI. Reciprocal Rights and Duties of Mother and Children. VII. Divorce.

12mo, cloth, $1. Half bound, $1.25.

BASTIAT. SOPHISMS OF PROTECTION.

By FREDERIC BASTIAT. With Preface by HORACE WHITE. Cloth. Price $1.00.

REEVES. The Students' Own Speaker. A Manual of Oratory By Paul Reeves. 12mo, boards, 75 cts.; cloth, 90 cts.

The "Student's Own Book," by Paul Reeves, which forms the first of the Handy-Book Series, is notable among other points in giving "a good deal for the money." The amount of matter in this book, which is in clear and neat, though small type, fully equals that in other books of twice the size and cost. It contains many new pieces not to be found in any of the school text-books. It aims to meet the wants of a large number outside of the school-room, while it is also well adapted for school use.

The *Philadelphia Inquirer* says of it:

"The general rules laid down, and the suggestions thrown out, are excellent, while the pieces furnished for declamation are well chosen. The book is one deserving a wide circulation."

Another good authority says:

"We have never before seen a collection so admirably adapted for its purpose. Prose and verse, humor, eloquence, description, alteration, burlesque discourse of every kind. . . . For schools, clubs, and fireside amusement, it will be found an almost inexhaustible source of entertainment. . . . The instruction . . . is sensible and practical."

RICHARDSON. House Building. From a Cottage to a Mansion. A Practical Guide to Members of Building Societies, and all interested in selecting or Building a House. By C. J. Richardson, Architect, author of "Old English Mansions." With 600 illustrations. Crown 8vo, cloth extra, $3.50.

RITCHIE. The Romance of History—France. By Leitch Ritchie. Illustrated. 12mo, cloth extra, $2.50.

ROGERS. Social Economy. By Prof. E. Thorold Rogers (Tooke Professor of Economic Science, Oxford, England), editor of "Smith's Wealth of Nations." Revised and edited for American readers. 12mo, cloth, 75 cts.

This little volume gives in the compass of 150 pages, concise yet comprehensive answers to the most important questions of Social Economy. The relations of men to each other, the nature of property, the meaning of capital, the position of the laborer, the definition of money, the work of government, the character of business, are all set forth with clearness and scientific thoroughness. The book, from its simplicity and the excellence of its instruction, is especially adapted for use in schools, while the information it contains is of value and interest to all classes of readers.

"It is this sort of knowledge that is contained in Prof. Rogers' book, which we cannot too highly recommend to the use of teachers, students, and the general public."—*American Athenæum.*

ROGERS. The Poetical Works of Samuel Rogers. Including "Italy," "Columbus," "Pleasures of Memory," etc., with portrait. 12mo, cloth extra, $1.50; half calf, $3.50.

SEGUIN. A Manual of Thermometry. For Mothers, Nurses, and all who have charge of the Sick and the Young. By Edward Seguin, M.D. 12mo, cloth, 75 cts.

www.ingramcontent.com/pod-product-compliance
Lightning Source LLC
Chambersburg PA
CBHW020230030726
47497CB00009B/3034